D1766093

Sherlock Holmes – The Baker Street Epilogue

Another collection of previously unknown cases from the extraordinary career of Mr. Sherlock Holmes

Mark Mower

Paperback ISBN 978-1-78705-706-7
ePub ISBN 978-1-78705-707-4
PDF ISBN 978-1-78705-708-1

Published in the UK by MX Publishing
335 Princess Park Manor, Royal Drive,
London, N11 3GX
www.mxpublishing.co.uk
Cover design by Brian Belanger

Contents

Preface

Dear readers - Following the successful publication of *Sherlock Holmes: The Baker Legacy* four years ago, you have once again challenged me to gather together another selection of previously unknown Holmes and Watson cases from the prized collection of stories I inherited from my uncle in 1939. This is my response to your polite requests – *Sherlock Holmes: The Baker Street Epilogue*. I trust you will embrace it as positively as you did for the three previous volumes.

Earlier this year we witnessed an audacious crime which would have been worthy of the attention of our heroes. The villains behind the Eastcastle Street robbery in the West End held up a Post Office van and got away with £287,000 – the nation's largest post-war heist. It is widely believed that the criminal mastermind behind this stunt is a well-connected and dapper gangster from London. And yet, no robbers have been arrested to this point. Oh, how we long for the deductive capabilities of the Great Detective!

This fine country of ours has changed radically since 1881 when Watson was first introduced to Holmes by his friend Stamford. Had they not met and become the closest of friends our collective memory of the world's greatest sleuth would be significantly diminished. Yet with the preservation of the good doctor's narratives, we can relive that era and retrace those seventeen steps to their Baker Street apartment. The publication of every new story enables us to escape - if only for a brief period - from the humdrum nature of our post-war reality. As Vincent Starrett put it so articulately in his poem *221B*:

"...Here though the world explodes, these two survive,

And it is always eighteen ninety-five."

As before, these new stories are more overlooked gems. From the challenge of *The Recalcitrant Rhymester* to the unsettling affair of *The Bewildered Blacksmith*, there is, as ever, much to entertain and enthral us.

As you may have ascertained from its title, this book is likely to serve as the final volume of stories from my uncle's cherished collection. I think it unlikely that I will be minded to release another book, but who knows! The fact that you have encouraged me to publish four books to date demonstrates clearly that there is no loss of appetite when it comes to new Sherlock Holmes stories. Long may that continue!

So, dim the gas lamp, get settled in your favourite wing-backed chair, and steady yourself with a glass of your favourite tipple. It promises to be a long night. For, as always, *"The game is afoot!"*

Christopher Henry Watson, MD

Bexley Heath, Kent – 18th September 1952

1. The Curse of Cuttleborough

It was in the early part of 1883 that I joined the Norwood Cricket Club and was fortunate in being picked to play in half a dozen matches throughout the long summer of that memorable year. And despite the limitations on my agility, brought about by my persistent war wounds, I always seemed to give a good account of myself being no slouch when it came to batting.

Sherlock Holmes would occasionally accompany me to the Albert Road ground, cheering enthusiastically from the clubhouse whenever I took my place at the crease. And it was during that same summer that he became acquainted with another frequent visitor to the ground, the famous amateur cricketer, W. G. Grace. I was already on good terms with the busy medical practitioner, for he had asked me three or four times if I might stand in for him and visit some of the patients he regularly attended to.

Yet it came as something of a surprise to receive an unexpected visit from the man at our Baker Street apartment in the November of that year. The tall, slim, and clean-shaven thirty-five-year-old cut quite a figure in his neatly-tailored frockcoat and expensive top hat – a distinctly different vision from the huge frame, swarthy features, and bushy beard he was later to be known for. Mrs. Hudson seemed all aflutter in announcing his arrival, taking his hat and coat from him, and then asking if he would like a cup of tea. Holmes and I greeted the fellow warmly and my colleague was quick to direct him towards the armchair nearest the fire.

"Dr. Grace, this is indeed a pleasure," intoned Holmes, taking his own seat and reaching for his churchwarden and tobacco. "I hope you will not mind me smoking while you outline the particulars of this troubling matter at Cuttleborough Manor."

Our visitor's quick dark eyes took on a wary expression. "Is the reason for my visit so obvious and transparent?" he asked in his strong Bristolian burr. "I know you to be an accomplished detective, Mr. Holmes, but had not expected you to be quite so quick-witted! As for your pipe and tobacco, smoke away – I'm not your doctor."

Holmes ignored the directness of the response and sought to explain his own frankness, while returning the pipe and tobacco to the side table by his chair: "I'm sorry if my remark seemed a trifle brusque. But in meeting you previously, I was struck by your endless vitality and breeziness. Today you present yourself with a troubled expression and a distinctly downbeat tone. Ordinarily you are precise and fastidious in your attire, yet today I note that you are wearing odd socks. I know from my conversations with Dr. Watson that your medical priorities caused you to miss a recent Gentlemen versus Players match – the first such fixture you have been absent from since 1867. All of which leads me to believe that some significant matter is weighing heavily upon you."

He pointed briefly towards a copy of *The Times* which sat on the table near the window. "It is a matter of public record that you have, in recent months, been treating a peer of the realm for an undiagnosed illness. That the death of the man in question was announced in the press some days ago, provides me with a strong indication that it could be this matter which has been at the forefront of your mind. And the letterhead bearing the name 'Cuttleborough Manor' - which is protruding from the right pocket of your frockcoat - provides the final confirmation. I believe that is the ancestral home of the late Earl of Rumburgh?"

Dr. Grace was momentarily speechless, but then smiled broadly and opened his arms in an expansive gesture. "I pride myself on my own observational skills and my professional ability to diagnose the hidden maladies and ailments of my patients. Eleven years of medical training has equipped me to do so. But you have a rare and unique talent, and you seem to play it with a straight bat. I feel even more confident that you are, indeed, the man to assist me, aided, of course, by this fine fellow here."

Grace's unexpected nod towards my own role touched me instantly. I was about to respond when the door opened, and Mrs. Hudson entered carrying a tea tray. "Your refreshments, gentlemen. And a plate of freshly-baked biscuits for our distinguished guest."

"Thank you, Mrs. Hudson," said Holmes. "Our landlady is something of a cricket fanatic, doctor," he added, as if some explanation were required.

"Evidently," replied our visitor, with a beaming smile. "That is exceedingly kind of you, Mrs. Hudson. I am very partial to a decent biscuit."

"Thank you, sir! Glad to be of service." She left the room with a distinct spring in her step.

When we had distributed the tea and biscuits and resumed our seats, Holmes returned to the matter at hand. "I would be grateful if you could outline the details of the affair. I take it that you have some concerns as to the nature of the Earl's demise?"

"Yes," replied the doctor. "But I will get to that in due course. The letter that you have observed in my pocket is an invitation to attend the man's funeral, which has been arranged for next week. I think it only fair to explain to you the full details of my association with Richard Silverton, otherwise known as the Third Earl of Rumburgh. After the events of the last two months, I had not expected to receive such an invitation."

He took a large gulp of his tea and set the cup down on the saucer by his side. "As a child, I lived with my parents and siblings in a place called Downend House, near Bristol. After attending a couple of early preparatory schools, I was eventually enrolled as a pupil at a day school known as Ridgway House. There was nothing remarkable about the school, and – truth be told – I could not claim to be an overly scholarly pupil. But it afforded me a decent enough education and a curriculum which included plenty of outdoor activities, so I was content enough. However, what made my time there particularly enjoyable was my close friendship with young Richard Silverton, the second son of the then Earl, who owned the small, centuries-old, estate of Cuttleborough Manor which sat close to the school.

"Richard, or 'Dickie', as I knew him, was a rebellious, headstrong, and thoroughly likeable character, who shared my love of outdoor games and was always up for a bit of mischief making. Like me, he found many of his academic studies tedious, and was never happier than when we were climbing trees, playing conkers, or donning our cricket whites for the school's first eleven. His father, then a prominent peer and leading Parliamentarian, despaired at Dickie's wayward habits, but seemed content not to send him to a more prestigious school because the family's long-term hopes lay with Dickie's brother, Robert, who was destined to inherit the estate and peerage by virtue of being the eldest son.

"The summer holidays were a particular favourite of ours, and until I left the school in my fourteenth year, I would spend every July and August as a permanent guest at the manor. Dickie and I were inseparable, and alongside Timothy Tranter, the son of the estate's gardener and housekeeper, we formed an unlikely posse, building camps and generally running riot. On one occasion, Dickie saved me from drowning in the village pond, an act which would forever place me in his debt.

"When he was 10, Dickie's dear mother, Dorothea, died of consumption. He was overwhelmingly distraught and struggled to come to terms with the loss. He became more wayward and would constantly challenge his father's authority. And it was at this point that he first told me about *the curse of Cuttleborough*."

To this point, Holmes had been stretched back in his chair, his hands steepled, and his eyes closed. At once, he sat upright, opened his eyes, and looked directly at the doctor: "A *curse*, you say? What sort of curse?"

"I am almost loath to mention it. For as a medical man, impervious to most irrational convictions, I would ordinarily pay scant attention to such seemingly superstitious claptrap. But at the time, I remember being chilled by Dickie's wholehearted belief in the inevitability of the curse. And in the light of recent events, I have begun to wonder increasingly about the debilitating effects that a misplaced belief might have on a man's body and mind, and whether this could actually result in premature death."

"Without doubt," I opined. "I have seen it myself, particularly among some of my elderly patients. If they are firmly of the belief that their time has come and any medical intervention on my part is futile, their demise can be swift. Conversely, where I am able to convince them that they have all to live for, and a treatment can facilitate such an outcome, they will normally rally and surprise me with their longevity – even if that course of treatment has but a placebo effect."

I could see Holmes was looking at me with a degree of scepticism. "Let us hear the nature of this supposed curse before we start jumping to conclusions about its potential to kill," he said with a wry smile, once again picking up his pipe and tobacco.

Dr. Grace continued: "Cuttleborough Manor was built in the seventeenth century on land previously owned by a non-conformist *wise woman*, known locally as 'Mother Lackland'. The church authorities had tired of her use of homespun potions and hedgerow remedies to treat the poor, sick, and infirm of the village, and had threatened her with prosecution if she did not stop practising her 'witchcraft'. When she refused to do so, they brought her before the Bishop of Bristol. Found 'guilty' of all the charges against her, Mother Lackland was hanged from a gibbet erected on her own land – the same plot which was later bought by the Silverton family. It was said that she had cursed the land prior to her execution; specifically announcing that any family which made their home there would be *damned to extinction*."

"And the family were inclined to believe this?" The cynicism in Holmes's voice was barely concealed.

"More than inclined," countered Grace. "In the seventeenth century, the Silverton family was well rooted in all the counties of south-west England. They held manorial lands in a dozen locations and their progeny could be found in the Royal Court, in Parliament, the judiciary, the clergy and the armed forces. In the two and a half centuries since that time, their numbers have dwindled as the family name has been associated unerringly with misfortune, tragedy, fatality, and loss – events which were attributed to the curse. So much so, that Dickie was the last surviving male descendent of that once esteemed family. With his passing, the Silverton line has effectively ended."

Holmes was at once intrigued. "Indeed! And what will now happen to their residual wealth and lands?"

Dr. Grace smiled uneasily. "Therein lies another mystery of an earthlier nature. Dickie's father, Ronald, inherited the last remnants of the Silverton estate – a small manor house, a sizeable portion of farmland, and a dozen tenants who worked the land. When he became an Earl, the family believed that their fortunes had changed. And with two healthy sons, Ronald had high hopes that the Silverton line would continue and thrive with the hereditary title. But the man himself died in a horse-riding accident ten years ago and his heir, Robert, passed away earlier this year having suffered from a rare blood disorder.

"When he left school, Dickie became even more rebellious in his attitude towards his father. He was the hereditary 'spare' with no role and little ambition. He spent his time drinking in the village and falling out with the estate staff. He and I went our separate ways, and he also had a major falling out with our friend Timothy Tranter, who was encouraged to leave Cuttleborough and find work in London. Eventually, under pressure from his father, Dickie accepted a commission in the army and was posted overseas. That was where he spent the last 15 years, learning to control his temper and having no desire to return to the country of his birth. But when word came that his brother Robert had passed, Dickie resigned his commission and finally made the passage back from India.

"As the new Earl of Rumburgh, he returned to his family home and set about making changes to the estate, much to the chagrin of his staff and tenants. He had hopes of taking his seat in Parliament but found travel increasingly difficult. In short, while he had always been in excellent health, he had contracted a debilitating disease while in India which now began to take its toll on his physical condition. Terrified that this was further evidence of the family curse, he contacted me in April, desperately hoping that my medical knowledge and expertise could cure him and refusing to see any other doctor. For five months, I made repeated journeys from London to Cuttleborough, struggling to diagnose the nature of his malaise, and all without success. By September, he was completely bedbound, and I gave him but days to live."

I interjected. "And yet, he did not die."

Grace regarded me keenly with a look of some despair. "No, it was most odd, particularly in the light of what happened next."

"Which was?" asked Holmes, with just a hint of agitation.

"At that point, his communications with me ceased. I received no further telegrams and my repeated attempts to visit the manor were unsuccessful, with the housekeeper telling me that the Earl wished to have no further association with me. I wondered if he felt I had failed him and decided with much reluctance to accede to his request and remain in London."

Holmes sent a plume of grey smoke towards the fireplace and pointed the stem of his churchwarden towards our visitor. "You will forgive me, doctor, but I am still struggling to understand what will now happen to the family estate."

If Grace had been offended by my friend's dismissive remark, he showed no sign of it. "Indeed, Mr. Holmes, I fear that I am still playing into the long grass. Let me give you a fair sight of the ball."

A bemused grin played across my colleague's face as he once again settled back into his chair.

"I had not expected Dickie to survive beyond the end of September, and hearing nothing further from him at that time, took to scanning the society columns each day, believing that some announcement of his passing would be evident. So, you can imagine my surprise when, during the second week of October, I saw a small piece reporting that Richard Silverton, the Third Earl of Rumburgh, had attended Parliament for the first time, during which he had presented his *letters patent* to the Crown Office as evidence of his right to take his seat in the House of Lords. Stunned, I searched through all the main newspapers to see if there was any mention of the Earl's health but drew a blank.

"Against my professional judgement, I hoped that Dickie had pulled off a miraculous recovery. And I waited in the expectation that I might receive some message from him in the days that followed. Yet none was forthcoming. And then, earlier this week, the papers reported that he had finally passed away. I took the first train down to Bristol and visited Cuttleborough Manor. The housekeeper was curt in receiving me. She offered me no refreshment and refused my request to see the body of my friend which had yet to be laid to rest. The death had apparently been certified by a doctor from the village.

"Just before I left, her husband - the gardener – arrived. He seemed unsettled by my appearance. And in the short time I spent with the pair, I found myself asking what would happen to the estate now that Dickie had gone. My enquiry provoked a strange response from Mr. Tranter. With what looked like an expression of some glee, he looked me straight in the eye and announced that everything had been left to them as 'the original, loyal and last-remaining servants of the Silverton family.' I was staggered and knew in that instant that something was amiss."

"Why do you say that?" asked Holmes.

"Because Dickie had no regard for the couple. As a child, he was constantly moaning about them and hated the way they scolded their son for wanting to play with us. They were always berating him and never missed an opportunity to let his father know about his unruly behaviour. When he returned from India, he admitted that he was considering dismissing 'the loathsome Tranters' who had made his life such a misery when his mother had died."

"Perhaps they were more supportive of him during those final few weeks of his life," I suggested.

"I doubt that. I felt it my duty to confide in them during the summer that their employer was seriously ill and might not survive into the autumn. They did not seem surprised or even vaguely sympathetic. In fact, their reaction – or lack of it – caused me to wonder whether they might be doing something to contribute to his illness. So much so, that I took several blood samples and tested for a variety of poisons, all without result."

"I see," replied Holmes. "So, what is it that you would have us do in investigating the case? It should be simple enough to verify the circumstances surrounding your friend's death, and I daresay that we can ascertain whether a valid will exists to support Mr. Tranter's claim."

"Simply that, Mr. Holmes. You have a nose for these things. I do not say that any great crime has been committed but cannot help thinking that poor old Dickie has been bowled a googly. Something is amiss." With that, he withdrew the paperwork from the right pocket of his frockcoat and passed it to my friend. "If the Earl did not wish to have any further association with me, why should the housekeeper now write inviting me to attend the funeral?"

Holmes cast a quick glance at the letter and smiled enigmatically. "Why, indeed? Now, a final question for you. During your visits to the manor, when you were still attending to the ailing Richard Silverton, did you ever meet or see Timothy Tranter?"

With some bemusement, Grace furrowed his eyebrows. "*No*. Why do you ask?"

"Well, it struck me that the man might have put in an appearance given your childhood friendship – the three of you having once formed, as you described earlier, 'an unlikely posse.'"

"No, I never saw the fellow. I did ask Mrs. Tranter how he was doing. She said he had his own Hackney carriage and had worked for many years as a London cabbie. She was evidently proud of him."

"No doubt," replied Holmes quickly, placing his pipe to one side and rising from his chair. "I will be pleased to take on your case, for it certainly has some features of interest. Tomorrow is Friday," he mused, "and the funeral is next Tuesday. I am confident that Dr. Watson and I can get to the bottom of this affair by then."

"Close of play on Monday would be perfect, gentlemen. I will be dining at Lord's Cricket Ground that evening, if you would care to join me? I plan to travel to the funeral the following morning."

"Then we will meet you at Lord's around eight o'clock," answered Holmes, making for the door of the study. "I will just shout down to Mrs. Hudson who will retrieve your hat and overcoat. A good day to you, sir."

A short while later Holmes and I reflected on the unexpected visit. My colleague did not say much, but I could tell he was enthusiastic about the case and already formulating a plan: "We have time for a light luncheon, Watson. And I suggest we pack and travel down to Cuttleborough later this afternoon. In between, I have a few immediate enquiries to make before we leave London."

****

We set off from Paddington a little later than planned for the journey to Bristol Temple Meads. It was busy on the Great Western train and we were forced to share our first-class apartment with a trainee priest and a barrister from Tunbridge Wells. As it turned out, both men proved to be lively company and the time passed remarkably quickly. Outside the station we hired a pony and trap for the short journey to Cuttleborough where we booked ourselves into the *Valiant Sailor* public house in the centre of the village.

The clientele at the inn proved to be no less entertaining than our railway companions, and over a filling meal of venison, cabbage, and mashed potatoes, we learned more about the Silverton family and their recent history. The first Earl of Rumburgh had been well regarded by the locals, for he had made every effort to pay his estate workers a fair wage and had supported their families in times of ill health. By contrast, his eldest son Robert had gambled his way through a fair proportion of the family's wealth and had sought to reduce costs on the estate by cutting wages and raising the rents of his tenants. Richard Silverton came in for no less criticism given the changes he had made to the estate throughout the summer. No one seemed to be saddened by the recent announcement of his death.

After a late breakfast the next day, we walked the half-mile to Cuttleborough Manor. It was a bright but brutally cold day, and I was glad I had remembered to pack a thick scarf and gloves in addition to my fur-lined overcoat. Even Holmes seemed to be feeling the chill, as he turned his head towards me a couple of times to shield his face from the biting northerly wind. We reached the impressive wrought iron gateway of the estate, atop of which was a large metal plate displaying the Silverton coat of arms. Ahead of us lay a long gravel drive to the manor house.

It was with some relief that we finally reached the sheltered porchway of the manor house and I stepped up to knock on the heavy oak door before us. It took a good three or four minutes before the door was opened with a distinct and prolonged creak. We were faced with a pudgy, stern-looking, woman, whose only redeeming feature was her intensely green eyes, which were fixed upon us inviting further explanation. "*Yes?*"

Holmes sought to oblige the housekeeper. "Good morning, Mrs. Tranter. My name is Sherlock Holmes, and this is my colleague, Dr. John Watson. We are here in connection with the recent demise of His Lordship, the Third Earl of Rumburgh. I wonder if we might ask you a few questions about the nature of his death."

The formal nature of his speech and demeanour seemed to have an immediate influence on the woman, whose features first softened and then took on a look of some disquiet. "I would be pleased to assist you, sirs, but would prefer it if my husband were present. He is, as we speak, in the kitchen. I will just check that he is comfortable to receive guests at the present time." With that, she turned and headed off down the main entrance hall.

We stood in front of the open door watching her depart. I could not help but whisper: "It seems our gardener has settled into the life of a country squire rather quickly!"

"Indeed," retorted Holmes. "I have no doubt he will oblige us - when he is ready!'

Some moments later, the housekeeper returned and beckoned us in. It was a dark and tired looking entrance hall which greeted us. A once-grand setting that had clearly seen better days. One or two sizeable oil paintings and a faded medieval tapestry graced the panelled walls, beyond which led a corridor into the heart of the house. The kitchen proved to be at the far end of this through an arched doorway. The room was surprisingly light and spacious compared to the corridor from which we had come and the floor beneath our feet was composed of odd-shaped and irregularly laid flagstones which were almost certainly original. Mr. Tranter sat at one end of a large refectory table which filled about a fifth of the space to our left. He made no effort to rise as we were directed by his wife towards some chairs at opposite end of the table.

"And how may I help you, gentleman? My wife Jinny tells me that you have some questions about the late Earl. I hope you're not journalists – we've had more than enough of them sniffing around lately." He took a large swig from the tankard he had in his right hand and then wiped his lips with the back of his left.

"We are not journalists," replied Holmes. He answered without looking at the man and his keen eyes continued to scan the room. His gaze settled on a Welsh dresser to our right as he added, "but I am a private enquiry agent."

What the gardener made of this I could not tell, but his wife appeared to believe that this conferred some sort of 'official' status to our visit. She sat down on a chair to our right and said, somewhat timorously, "we'd best answer the gentleman straight, Geoffrey. What is it you'd be *enquiring about* exactly?"

Holmes looked at her. "The newspapers said that the Earl died of a heart attack, but I understand he had been ill for some months, from the moment he returned from India."

The housekeeper was clearly unnerved. "You are well informed, sir. Young Richard – the late Earl – was very poorly when he came back to us. We looked after him as best we could, but he was certainly out of sorts."

"And he was attended to initially by a doctor?"

"That's right – a Dr. Grace. He was one of Richard's old schoolfriends."

"Bit of a show-off, that man," added Geoffrey Tranter, without further explanation.

Holmes ignored the comment. "I believe Dr. Grace stopped attending to the Earl in early September. Why was that?"

Jinny Tranter answered him a little more confidently. "They had something of a falling out. After which, Richard refused to have him in the house."

"I see. And do you know why they quarrelled?"

"Yes. When he first returned from India, Richard had a visit from Mr. Brimblecombe, the family's solicitor. He was keen for him to make a will, seeing as he was the new Earl and all, and no provision had been made for what might happen in the event of his death. You see, he had no offspring of his own and...well, the family has had its fair share of unexpected deaths in the past. For some reason, Richard dragged his heels in addressing the matter and Dr. Grace seemed to take exception to this. He was constantly reminding Richard of the need to sort out the legalities."

I interjected. "Why would he do that - Grace, I mean? He's a doctor, not a solicitor."

"I guess he knew the Earl's days were numbered," replied Mr. Tranter. "Wanted to line his own pockets."

"That's a very scandalous remark, sir! What are you suggesting?"

It was Mrs. Tranter who responded, a little more tactfully. "Well, we can't be sure, doctor, but from the few words Richard said about the matter, we got the impression that Dr. Grace had hoped to be the beneficiary of Richard's will."

I was angry at the suggestion, believing that I knew enough of Grace's character and integrity to be certain that this was all poppycock. Holmes placed a reassuring hand on my left forearm, signalling for me not to say anything further, before then speaking himself. "Well, regardless of what he might or might not have said, it seems that the Earl had other intentions as regards his legacy. I believe that the two of you are now in line to inherit the Silverton fortune..."

Mrs. Tranter shifted in her seat. "That's right. Mr. Brimblecombe is sorting everything out and does not anticipate any difficulties."

"And Mr. Brimblecombe is based where?"

"In the village. He has an office in the high street."

"Were you surprised to find out that everything had been left to you?"

The question prompted a bullish response from Mr. Tranter. "No. The family line had come to an end. Why shouldn't the likes of us benefit?"

Holmes disregarded the man for a second time and merely stood up and walked over to the dresser. Mr. Tranter watched him quizzically and then glanced towards his wife.

"How has your son, Timothy, responded to the news? He must be delighted to learn of your unexpected windfall. I take it that this is a photograph of him, alongside young Richard and William Grace?" He turned to face Mrs. Tranter. In his right hand he held what looked to be a small *carte de visite*.

The housekeeper's face had taken on a reddish hue and she began to stumble on her words. "He...he was very pleased for us. And yes, that's...that's a picture of the three boys when they were 13. Always playing together on the estate. Like three peas in a pod..."

She stopped abruptly as Holmes passed the photograph to me. It was a small visiting card set within an ornate silver frame. Three dark-haired boys were sat together on a wooden bench, all dressed in their cricket whites. It looked to have been taken on a sunny summer's day. Each boy was smiling, and I had to scrutinise the face of each for some seconds to realise which was W. G. Grace.

"You were saying, Mrs. Tranter..."

"Sorry, yes... that picture was taken in 1862. The first Earl commissioned it and let us have a copy. He always said it was his favourite photograph..."

"The boys certainly look happy. Were they good friends?"

"The very best, sir," she said wistfully. "Timmy was never happier than when Richard broke up for the summer holidays and Grace came to stay."

"And you say they were all 13 years of age?"

"Yes, Timmy was a month older than Richard and three or four months older than Grace. They were all bright lads, but my Timmy was the best behaved and most capable of the three..."

"That's right – and he didn't have the schooling or the privileges the others got. Might have been more than a cabbie if he had."

"And will Timothy be at the funeral next week?" enquired Holmes, rather obliquely.

Mrs. Tranter's expression was suddenly as stern as it had been on the doorstep. "Oh, yes, he'll be there..."

I placed the framed photograph down on the table. Mrs. Tranter retrieved it somewhat territorially and rose to take it back to where it had originally sat on the dresser.

My friend waited for her to return to the table: "Who attended to the Earl after he suffered the heart attack? Clearly, it was not Dr. Grace."

The gardener answered. "No. Doctor in the village. Chandler his name is."

"Thank you. And what about the funeral? Are the arrangements all in hand?"

Mrs. Tranter responded angrily. "We *are capable* of arranging such an event! It's not the first time we've had to. Birkett & Chapman, the undertakers, are assisting us. The funeral casket will be taken by hearse to the crypt of St. Michael's on Monday. Now, if you have no further questions, I would be grateful if you could leave us in peace!"

We thanked them for their time and the housekeeper escorted us back the way we had come. As we stepped out into the porch, the front door was slammed shut behind us.

"We seem to have hit more than a few raw nerves, Watson!" said Holmes under his breath. "A very useful and productive interview, I'd say."

We began to make our way back down the gravel drive. I had little doubt that our every step was being observed. "Well, they certainly seemed very tetchy," I agreed, "but I'm not sure we discovered anything we didn't already know."

"On the contrary, my friend. The nature of this affair has become much clearer. And we also know where to continue our enquiries."

"Ah, that I did note. For we have the names of both the family solicitor and the doctor who certified the death."

"Precisely. And I believe that a visit to the parish church of St. Michael's might prove useful. I will do that, as well as speaking to Mr. Brimblecombe and the undertakers. Could I suggest that you consult with Dr. Chandler to learn what you can?"

"Certainly."

"Then all being well, we will meet back at the hotel sometime later this afternoon."

****

I had to wait over two hours before I could speak to Dr. Chandler. His small medical practice was situated beside a busy bakery and coffee shop, so I took the opportunity to sit in the toasty interior and enjoy some freshly baked rolls and a delicious cheese scone. The shop appeared to operate as an informal reception area for the surgery, and the manager was quite comfortable to take messages for the doctor as people passed through. He also seemed to know something of Chandler's daily schedule, for he explained that the man was busy making house calls, but would no doubt see me on his return. I could do little but wait.

When Dr. Chandler returned to the surgery he was more than willing to see me. I got the impression he rarely met or conversed with other doctors, especially those of my age – for while I was then in my earlier thirties, I guessed him to be in his mid-eighties. He proved to be both genial and open in sharing his observations on the Earl's demise but seemed to be unacquainted with much of the man's earlier life. He admitted that it was the first time he had been called upon to attend to anyone in the Silverton family, for they had always used the services of expensive doctors in Bristol.

He described the death as "straightforward" – a simple heart attack which had most likely resulted from a combination of over exertion, smoking and excessive alcohol consumption. Given the Earl's age and social status, the local coroner had directed Chandler to carry out a full *post mortem*. This had revealed dozens of atheroma – small, but excessive build ups of fatty plaque – which had clogged and narrowed the man's arteries exposing him to the constant risk of a stroke or heart failure.

I was a little surprised to hear this, for I had understood the late Earl to be suffering from an undiagnosed illness which he had contracted abroad. Dr. Grace had also said that prior to that Silverton had always been in excellent health. I knew Grace to be an excellent surgeon and felt certain that he would have had no trouble in diagnosing the early onset of heart disease. I then asked Chandler if he had seen evidence of any other infection, tissue breakdown, or blood poisoning. He answered in the negative.

I was conscious of taking up too much of the amiable doctor's time, so asked him, finally, if there was anything at all which had struck him as odd when carrying out the autopsy. He thought for a moment, and then smiled. "Yes, the man's pallor was rather curious. For a fellow who had spent so many years in India, he was surprisingly pale. And as a senior officer in Her Majesty's Army, whom I imagined to be unused to hard physical labour, his hands were severely calloused, as if he'd had a lifetime of manual work."

I thanked the good doctor and left the surgery, making my way back through the village to the *Valiant Sailor*. Holmes had not returned to the public house, so I spent half an hour reading in my room and mulling over what Chandler had told me. *Was it possible that Richard Silverton had made an astonishing recovery from a debilitating south-Asian illness, only to be struck down by a heart attack at thirty-five years of age?* Possible, yes, but unlikely, I concluded.

Holmes was very chipper when I met up with him a little after one-thirty that afternoon. We sat in the tap room of the inn warming ourselves before a large log fire and sharing a jug of locally brewed ale. Holmes had resorted to his briar pipe while I was enjoying a small cigarillo.

"So, the consultation with Dr. Chandler raised more questions than it provided answers," said Holmes suddenly, as if reading my mind.

"Yes," I conceded. "How did you know that?"

"You told me that you returned around one o'clock and went straight to your room. When travelling you are something of an avid reader and always have a book packed for any idle moments you encounter. Ordinarily, you can be absorbed in a good novel for two or three hours, yet today you were unable to settle and came down here to the bar after little more than 30 minutes. That you have been preoccupied is evident from the small whisky glass to your side. I would say that you have taken only one or two small sips of the single malt. And when I asked you if you would care to share a jug of ale with me, you consented immediately, as if forgetting you already had a drink. When we parted, you had but one visit to make, so I am confident in concluding that it must have been the information given to you by Dr. Chandler that has prompted this unusual introspection on your part."

I had to acknowledge that he was correct and then shared with him all that the doctor had imparted. He was not in the least bit surprised and responded accordingly: "Excellent. Then my working hypothesis has proved to be accurate!"

"And how were your own enquiries, productive?"

"Most certainly. Initially, I visited the undertakers, Birkett & Chapman. They assisted with the funeral arrangements for both the first and second Earls, so were the natural choice for this third burial. Mrs. Tranter ordered from them an expensive and solid casket which she said would befit a man of status. As part of their agreed role, the undertakers retrieved the body from Dr. Chandler's surgery and then prepared it for burial. The casket was then transported to Cuttleborough Manor as the housekeeper said that the late Earl had wanted his body to lie in repose for some days before being taken to the church. Birkett & Chapman have arranged for a hearse and six horses to carry the body to the crypt of St. Michael's on Monday in readiness for the funeral the next day."

It struck me that there was nothing at all revealing or remarkable about the arrangements which Holmes had described and yet he seemed highly animated in recounting the details. I then asked him about the solicitor. Once again, he was enthusiastic in the telling.

"Ah, well, it may interest you to know that Mr. Brimblecombe – a dependable and honest country solicitor if ever I met one – has vouched for the authenticity of the will. He confirmed what the Tranters told us - that he visited

Richard Silverton in April to suggest that the new Earl make a will. His advice was apparently ignored, and when the solicitor learned that Silverton was seriously ill and being attended to by Dr. Grace, he attempted to visit the manor two more times, again without success. Then, in mid-September, the Earl apparently sent word to Brimblecombe asking him to draw up a simple will to ensure that the Tranters would become his sole beneficiaries in the event of his death. A couple of days later he visited the manor and - in the presence of two independent witnesses – watched the Earl sign the required legal papers."

"Incredible!" I replied. "Then Geoffrey and Jinny Tranter are set to become the new owners of Cuttleborough Manor!"

"Oh, I did not say that, Watson! Remember, the adage: *there's many a slip 'twixt cup and lip*. There has been some skulduggery here, but there is still time to expose the nature of this devious plot."

He would not elaborate any further but continued his narrative. "My time at the church also proved to be fruitful. I spent some time talking to a Mr. Winterbourne, the aged gravedigger who is, as we speak, preparing the burial ground. He had some stories to tell about the Silverton family, in the light of which I then examined the church registers. I am now in possession of all the facts pertinent to this little mystery but will have to wait until the day of the funeral to finally lay the matter to rest, so to speak."

I have documented the many times that Holmes chose to be reticent about divulging what he had discovered and concluded in the midst of a case. This was another of those frustrating occasions when I had to wait for the great detective to declare his hand and reveal all. Despite my protestations, he refused to be drawn any further that day.

Later in the afternoon we caught a train from Bristol and arrived back in the capital at seven-thirty. Walking the mile or so from the station to Baker Street, we arrived at 221B in time to be treated to one of Mrs. Hudson's best meals – lamb cutlets, mint sauce, roast potatoes, and broccoli. Holmes gave me a sly wink as we ascended the seventeen stairs to our apartment having been told that the supper would be ready within ten minutes. "I had the good sense to wire ahead," he said, with a look of satisfaction.

****

The following Monday, we spent a pleasant evening in the company of Dr. W. G. Grace and his cricketing friends Billy Midwinter and Lord Harris, being wined and dined in the fashionable restaurant of the Lord's cricket ground. The amateur sportsman was in fine form, regaling us with colourful tales of his athletic endeavours. To that point, I had not realised that as well as being an extremely accomplished cricketer, the man also played for the Wanderers Football Club in Upper Norwood and some years earlier had been an outstanding hurdler.

Naturally, he asked about our enquiries. Holmes was able to tell him that we had made particularly good progress on our trip to Cuttleborough and the case would be resolved the following day, as we would both be travelling with the doctor to attend the funeral.

The Tuesday morning dawned bright and clear as we caught an early train from Paddington station. Dr. Grace looked a little bleary-eyed after his excesses the previous evening, but this did not diminish his natural energy and enthusiasm. And it was clear to me from the time that we had spent with him recently, that Holmes had a great deal of respect and affection for the fellow.

We arrived at the church of St. Michael's a good hour before the funeral service was due to begin. Grace insisted that we retire to the bar of a nearby hostelry in preparation for the proceedings, during which time Holmes slipped away on a mission of his own. I noted that he had pinned a small white ribbon to the lapel of his jacket.

After the customary memorial service, eight immaculately dressed pallbearers began to carry the casket out from the church towards the designated grave site – a sizeable rectangular area which had apparently served as the final resting place for the Silverton family since the seventeenth century. Some representatives of the Third Earl's regiment were in attendance to honour their former colleague, with a bugler set to end the burial with a rendition of the 'Last Post'.

In all, there were over a hundred people present at the funeral, including three or four recognisable peers who had come to show their respect. The Tranters were in the thick of the crowd, on one side of the grave. Both were tearful, and beside them stood others I assumed to be staff and workers from the estate. Some way off, I could also see Dr. Chandler, his hat removed, and his head bowed in respect. The Anglican minister leading the service was positioned at the head of the grave, poised to oversee the burial.

I had imagined that it would be after the funeral that Holmes would finally reveal to us the details of the Cuttleborough case. But I was to be wholeheartedly dumbfounded when I realised that the denouement was to occur there and then. As the casket was placed carefully on the ground beside the grave, a piercing whistle echoed across the graveyard and three uniformed constables advanced rapidly along the church path. They were followed by a fourth man bearing sergeant's stripes who continued to blow his police whistle until the detachment had reached the grave. At that point, seeing the white ribbon on Holmes's lapel, the officer stood to attention, saluted my colleague, and announced, "Sergeant Canning at your service, Mr. Holmes. Following your earlier telegram, the Chief Constable has directed that I am to give you any assistance you may require this afternoon."

My colleague thanked the sergeant, took a deep breath, and then addressed us all: "Lords, ladies and gentleman, you will have to excuse this outrageous intervention in what should have been a quiet and honourable funeral service for the Third Earl of Rumburgh. Regrettably, an audacious act of criminal deception has been perpetrated in the name of the late peer, which has required us to intercede and prevent this burial. These officers are from the Bristol Constabulary. Under their direction, I would ask that you leave the churchyard in an orderly and respectable fashion so that we may conclude our investigations. I am not at liberty to say anything further at this stage and would appreciate your willing cooperation in this most delicate of situations."

The vast majority of those present began to shuffle off quietly and a courteous silence continued for some seconds. One or two of the military men seemed a little perturbed by what they had witnessed and exchanged a few choice words under their breath before then falling in line. With a nod from Holmes, Sergeant Canning placed himself behind Geoffrey and Jinny Tranter, who had not moved. Within a few minutes the churchyard had been cleared by two of the police constables who then stood guard at the lychgate. In addition to the Tranters and the two other police officers, Holmes had directed that only myself, Dr. Grace, the Anglican minister, and one other man I did not recognise, should remain at the graveside.

Holmes spoke first to the cleric. "Apologies, Reverend Ives. I had no option but to put a stop to your service when I did. Given the course of events, I was not able to intervene earlier for fear that our culprits might realise that their nefarious scheme had been exposed."

The minister continued to look disgruntled. "I suppose I will have to take you at your word, sir, but I am struggling to see how I can condone such an action."

"All will become clearer as I explain," replied Holmes. He pointed to the man I had not recognised. "For those of you that do not know him, this is Mr. Winterbourne. He is a gravedigger for the parish of St. Michaels and has been most helpful in assisting me in recent days. Before the pallbearers arrived this afternoon, Winterbourne and I entered the crypt and examined the casket."

"By *examined*, I take it that you mean *you opened* the casket – is that correct, Mr. Holmes?" The clergyman seemed to be even more angry than he had been previously. "This is an act of desecration which is wholly unacceptable!"

It was the police sergeant who intervened. "Please let Mr. Holmes finish, sir! I am sure his actions were justified."

"Thank you, Sergeant." Holmes gestured towards Winterbourne who was evidently prepared for what was to come. With a small tool already in hand, the gravedigger began to move around the casket loosening all the fixings around its intricate construction. "If your constable could please assist Mr. Winterbourne in removing the lid of the casket, I think the Reverend Ives will understand why my action was warranted."

The two men lifted the lid of the casket free and placed it carefully beside the open coffin. All of us were now transfixed by what lay within. To one side was the body of a burly man in full military uniform, laid out on his back, with his eyes closed as if sleeping. On top of him and wedged in sideways on the opposite side of the casket, was a second cadaver which was facing towards the side wall. The body looked to be hideously emaciated and dressed only in a stained white nightshirt.

"Heaven's above!" exclaimed the Reverend Ives, echoing what all of us were thinking.

Dr. Grace stepped forward and stooped to examine the thinner of the two bodies. He turned towards Holmes and with a look of deep sorrow etched upon his pallid white features, spluttered, "It's Dickie Silverton!"

The Reverend Ives asked for the lid of the casket to be put back in place in deference to the deceased. Everyone then looked towards Holmes to explain the events which had led to this bizarre and macabre situation.

Holmes fixed his attention on Mr. and Mrs. Tranter. The latter stared back at him with a defiant look. "You cannot think that we had anything to do with this! We have been nothing but loyal servants to the Silvertons since first being employed at the manor."

"Indeed. Perhaps a little too loyal at times."

It was Mr. Tranter who now spoke. "What does that mean? Explain yourself, sir. I'll not have you berate my wife like that!"

"I'll happily do so, for there is much to tell. When I visited the churchyard last week and found Mr. Winterbourne digging this grave, I happened to ask him if he knew anything of the Silverton family. As it transpired, I could not have asked a better person, for our friend here was once a woodsman on the Cuttleborough estate. In that capacity, he got to hear a lot about what went on at the manor. And what he told me proved to be very revealing.

"This convoluted saga began over thirty-six years ago, when the married Ronald Silverton, later to become His Lordship, the First Earl of Rumburgh, was smitten by a young servant girl named Annie Reader. She was a maid of all work at the manor and was powerless to elude the amorous intentions of her employer. He was desperate to ensure that no one knew of his affair. Unfortunately for him, one person already did. For Annie had but one friend on the estate - the housekeeper, Mrs. Tranter, who had acted as something of an older sister to the girl when she joined the staff. One evening, in desperation, Annie confessed to Mrs. Tranter that she was with child. The housekeeper promised to help her.

"You see Mrs. Tranter saw an opportunity. She and her husband, the estate's gardener, wanted a family but had been unable to conceive a child of their own. One day, she boldly confronted her employer in his study, saying that she knew of his affair and the child that Annie Reader was carrying. She suggested a plan which would be in everybody's interest - a plan in which the young servant girl would leave the estate with a good reference and a generous sum of money. She would then be housed somewhere safely and discreetly for the remainder of her pregnancy. The housekeeper would accompany her and assist with the birth. After which time, the housekeeper would return to the estate claiming that the child was her own. Silverton agreed to the proposal, promising that the Tranters would also be recompensed and would retain their jobs for the remainder of his lifetime."

Mrs. Tranter interjected suddenly and with some bitterness: "Damnable lies! This is utter fiction."

"I'm afraid not. Until now, you would not have known that the whole of your conversation with Ronald Silverton was overheard by Mr. Winterbourne, who was clearing some wood outside the study at the time. But it was a revelation he kept to himself. You see, two days after this overheard conversation, Mr. Winterbourne was on a ship bound for Canada. He had secured a well-paid job as a lumberjack and hoped to prosper as a result. And for thirty years he lived a comfortable life there, not realising the significance of what he had listened to. He returned to the village a few years back, picking up whatever work he could. And until I asked him last week, he had never spoken to anyone about the affair."

The housekeeper was not to be outdone. "Hearsay, nonsense, all of it! What proof have you for any of this?"

"Well, in the light of Mr. Winterbourne's account, I took the opportunity to look through the church registers. I could not find any record relating to the baptism of a child named 'Reader' or 'Tranter', so can only assume that the child remained unbaptised so as not to draw any unwanted attention. Rather sadly, there was an entry in the burial register for an 'Annie Reader'. Clearly, she had died not long after having the baby. Whether that was the result of complications during the birth or something more sinister, we may never know."

Mr. and Mrs. Tranter remained silent, but Dr. Grace then spoke. "Holmes, this is all very melodramatic, but I think I speak for the rest of us when I say that we're still struggling to understand what all of this has to do with Dickie's death and his rather gruesome internment in someone else's coffin."

"I agree," intoned the Reverend Ives.

Holmes acknowledged their concerns. "I did say at the start that this was a convoluted affair. But I'm sure that you, of all people, will now have recognised that the child the housekeeper brought back to the manor to raise as her own, was Timothy Tranter, who you and Dickie played with during your fondly remembered summer holidays. When Dr. Watson and I visited the Tranters last week, we saw a small photograph of the three of you, taken when you were all 13 years old. The likeness between Richard Silverton and his illegitimate – and slightly older - stepbrother, Timothy, was unmistakable. Little wonder that it was, as Mrs. Tranter admitted, the first Earl's *favourite photograph.*

"Doctor, you told us yourself that after falling out with Richard, Timothy was forced to leave Cuttleborough and find work in London. We know that he became a cabbie with his own Hackney carriage. While I was still in London, I tried to find the man, without success. But I did discover that in early September Tranter's carriage was sold to another driver. My working hypothesis was that Timothy Tranter had returned to Cuttleborough Manor."

I had begun to see where all of this was leading. "He returned to the estate at the request of his adoptive parents when they told him what had happened at the manor!"

"Spot on, Watson! Richard Silverton, the newly ennobled Third Earl of Rumburgh, had finally succumbed to the mysterious south-Asian disease he had contracted in India. The Tranters knew that they now had another opportunity, one that was even more audacious than the adoption of Timothy. Since his return to England, the Earl had remained on the estate and had received very few visitors. With his illness, he became increasingly housebound. He was not even able to travel to London to take up his place in the House of Lords. Except for the visits from his childhood friend, Dr. Grace, the Earl lived as something of a recluse. As his health declined, the Tranters began to plot. They falsely told the doctor that Richard did not wish to see him anymore and took steps to prevent him from entering the manor. As he depended on them for everything, Richard had no way of contacting his friend or knowing why the doctor had stopped coming to Cuttleborough. And when he eventually died, in early September, they seized their chance.

"Timothy Tranter was told about the Earl's death. It is also likely that he was informed, for the first time, about his own parentage. Either way, he was brought into the plan to install him as a replacement for the Earl. His physical appearance was close enough to that of Richard Silverton to convince anyone he encountered that he *was* the peer. All but Dr. Grace of course. The Tranters continued to keep him away from the manor for fear that he might scupper their plans."

"This all makes perfect sense now," said Grace. "Kept *out in the field* you might say."

"Quite so, doctor. And emboldened by their early success, they then began to be more daring. Timothy contacted Mr. Brimblecombe, the family's solicitor, asking him to draw up a will, something the legal representative had been requesting for months. Brimblecombe and his two independent witnesses were there to see the man they believed to be the Earl sign the legal papers, ensuring that the Tranters would inherit everything in the event of their son's death. And in early October, Timothy made the trip to London to sit in the House of Lords for the first time. He took with him the Silverton *letters patent* which provided the documentary evidence of his hereditary peerage."

I looked across at the Tranters, both of whom now stood with their heads down, looking completely dejected. "It was certainly a wise move to get the will in place. They were not to know that Timothy had but a few weeks to live because of his advancing heart disease."

Mrs. Tranter mocked the assertion. "Of course we knew! It was Timmy who suggested getting the will prepared. His years as a hard-working cabbie had done him in. And like a true Silverton, he enjoyed his alcohol a little too much."

"It was curious," observed Holmes. "When we spoke to you last week, Mrs. Tranter, you kept referring to Timothy in the past tense. It strengthened my conviction that it was he who had died earlier this month."

"You'll never know how much that boy meant to me..."

Dr. Grace then asked. "After barring me from the manor, why did you then invite me to the funeral?"

Mr. Tranter regarded him with an expression of exasperation. "We knew that if anyone were to query how ill the Earl had been this year, you would give them chapter and verse on his slow decline and your futile attempts to save him. It just added to the plausibility of his death."

The doctor shot him a withering look. "How dare you!"

Sergeant Canning had been quiet to this point. He seemed to be struggling with some aspects of the narrative. "So, the uniformed man in the casket is the son of these two," he proffered, pointing his index finger towards the Tranters, "and having impersonated a dead man for what, two months, he dies himself?"

"That's right, Sergeant – he died of a heart attack. His body was then prepared by the funeral directors. They believed they were laying to rest the real earl and dressed him in full military regalia."

"Then why is the body of the *real earl* in there with him?!"

Holmes smiled gently. "When Richard Silverton died, the Tranters had to hide his body. They could not risk anyone

38

seeing the corpse. And while Timothy Tranter could impersonate the Earl, removing the need for them to account for the death, that still left them with the problem of what to do with the body. The death of their adopted son provided the solution. They had the undertakers bring the casket to the manor on the pretence that the late Earl wished his body to *lie in repose* before the burial. While there, they opened the casket and added the second cadaver. The Earl's frail condition prior to death probably meant that the corpse weighed a lot less than it might otherwise. They hoped the extra weight would not be noticed by the pallbearers."

"Very clever, Mr. Holmes! The Chief said you were as good a detective as Scotland Yard's finest!"

"I'll take that as a compliment," said Holmes, raising his eyebrows.

"While you are all congratulating yourselves," said Mrs. Tranter abruptly, "I would be grateful if you could tell me exactly what criminal charges you think you can bring against us. I'll grant you that we may be guilty of concealing a death, but we did not kill the Earl. And while Timothy was an imposter, he was entitled to take on the peerage by right, being the eldest son of an Earl. In that position he could also sign a will leaving the estate to us."

"I'm not sure that is how the law will view the matter. The will was not signed in his own name, so there is still the matter of fraud to contend with. In any case, I believe I am right in saying that an English peerage can only be inherited by a child who is born legitimate, to married parents."

"If there was a fraud, it was committed by Timothy, not us. And as for the laws on hereditary peerages, we will do everything to prove that it was his right to inherit the title!"

Sergeant Canning interposed. "Now, now! That will be matter for the judiciary. In the meantime, I have no option but to take the two of you into custody. We'll see what my inspector has to say about any charges that need to be brought against you."

So saying, the officer led the Tranters away. At the church gate, he directed the two constables standing guard to return to the grave. With the combined efforts of the constables, Mr. Winterbourne, Dr. Grace, and I, we managed to carry the casket back into the church where it was to wait until the Bristol Constabulary had arranged for a wagon or cart to transport it to a police station as evidence. Mr. Winterbourne volunteered to sit with the casket until such a time.

Back outside the church, the Reverend Ives continued to be furious about the drama which had been played out in his graveyard and stormed off towards the vicarage threatening repercussions from the Bishop. "Thank Heavens for that!" whispered Grace, watching the clergyman depart. He was something of a *biffer*. I'm pleased to see him dismissed."

Holmes laughed at the doctor's unexpected levity and then sought to console the man. "I'm sorry that your good friend should die in such circumstances. I know that we have resolved the case as I promised you, but the outcome can hardly be described as satisfactory. And at some point soon you will have to attend a second funeral."

The amateur cricketer nodded slowly. "Thank you, Mr. Holmes, and you, Dr. Watson. You are both fine fellows and I hope that we can maintain our friendship for many years to come. Let us leave this godforsaken village and make our way to Bristol. I favour catching the very first train back to London!"

We were all in agreement. Just before we set off, Holmes re-entered the church and thanked Mr. Winterbourne for his invaluable assistance on the case. He said that if the gravedigger ever found himself close to Baker Street, he should call in at 221B where he would always be welcome. The former lumberjack said he would do just that.

We did indeed maintain our friendship with Dr. Grace in the years that followed and were frequently invited to dine with him at Lord's. My sporting days were numbered, however, for by the summer of 1885 I felt it only fair to resign my membership of the Norwood Cricket Club as my batting scores had continued to tumble.

It was not to be the last time that we intervened to open a coffin prior to a planned burial. Some years later, Holmes insisted on that same course of action in a case I was to document as *The Disappearance of Lady Frances Carfax*.

And there was a curious postscript to the Cuttleborough case which we never shared with Dr. Grace. When Holmes was searching through the church records of St. Michael's he came across an entry in the marriage register which piqued his interest. Geoffrey Tranter had indeed married the woman who was to become housekeeper to the Silverton family. But who would have believed that the maiden name of his bride was 'Jinny *Lackland*'? Perhaps there had been something to *the curse of Cuttleborough* after all...

Notes: William Gilbert Grace MRCS LRCP (1848 to 1915) was a doctor and English amateur cricketer, often considered to be one of the sport's finest players. Batting and bowling for an incredible 44 seasons from 1865, he captained numerous teams, including England, Gloucestershire, and the Marylebone Cricket Club (MCC).

Dr. Watson's literary agent, Sir Arthur Conan Doyle, played in 71 matches for the Norwood Cricket Club between 1891 and 1894. He also played cricket for the MCC. Appearing in 10 first-class matches between 1900 and 1907, he took but one wicket – that of Dr. W. G. Grace, on 23rd August 1900. Conan Doyle would later write an obituary for Dr. Grace in *The Times* of 27th October 1915. It was entitled, *The Greatest of Cricketers*.

2. The Paradol Chamber

I have often reflected on the myriad of colourful characters that ascended the seventeen stairs to our Baker Street apartment. The footfall on those well-trodden steps truly represented all walks of life and the rich variety of our human species. So it was, that when Mr. Anthony Kildare was ushered into our quarters in the late-February of 1887, neither Holmes nor I raised so much as an eyebrow as he flounced in with a distinctly cavalier attitude and a flamboyant wardrobe to match.

Without waiting for an invitation to sit, he made straight for the nearest armchair and began to divest himself of his outer garments; a wide-brimmed purple hat, an orange knitted scarf with matching mittens and a vibrant blue tartan cape. In age, I guessed him to be in his late-fifties and the greying strands, rooted in his long, distinctly unkempt, brown hair, provided further assurance that he was no younger. It was also immediately apparent that he suffered from acute myopia, for I had never seen eyeglasses with thicker lenses.

"You, fellow", he bellowed, addressing Holmes abruptly, "am I to take it you are the detective chap that my personal secretary has told me so much about?" He cast a glance in my direction but seemed content to otherwise ignore my presence.

Holmes coughed and stifled what appeared to be a laugh. "Indeed I am. And this is my colleague Dr. John Watson. Now, Mr. Kildare, you have travelled with some haste from your quarters in Belgravia where your light breakfast of coffee and croissants was interrupted by the arrival of a significant letter in the first post - a missive on which you are now seeking my professional view. I already have something of a busy schedule today, so would be grateful if you could lift the veil on the nature of this particular correspondence."

The sarcasm was lost on our visitor who was momentarily stuck for words, something I imagined he was rarely susceptible to. When at last he managed to voice the concern he had been pondering, his tone was a little more conciliatory. "Sir, I apologise for my abrupt entrance, but how the deuce did you know all that?"

Holmes smiled and took to his favourite chair, nodding for me to do likewise. "The enamel badge on your cape proclaims you to be the President of the Prévost-Paradol Society, a social, literary and debating club set up to honour the French journalist and essayist Lucien-Anatole Prévost-Paradol - a talented man, who advocated for greater liberalism across Europe and took his own life in Washington in 1870, having been appointed as an envoy to the United States. While I never met the man myself, I have read some of his essays. I know the Society's headquarters are close to Grosvenor Gardens, and the fact that your cab pulled up opposite 221B and had, therefore, been travelling south to north, suggests that you came directly from your accommodation there. The small, flaky remnants of a croissant still adhere to your expensively tailored cape, lending weight to my theory that your breakfast was cut short and you finished what remained of the pastry while in a hastily hailed cab. The odour of strong coffee on your breath is a final, telling indicator that your meal was concluded only a short time ago. As for the letter, it is protruding from the left pocket of your frockcoat, which gives me both your name and a final confirmation of your address in Belgravia."

It was my turn to suppress a chuckle, for Mr. Kildare looked completely befuddled and merely removed the crumpled envelope from his pocket and passed it across to me, so that I might place it in Holmes's hands. Only when I had done so, did he seem to come to his senses with a quietly voiced, "thank you, Dr. Watson."

Holmes began to study the envelope and letter with characteristic zeal and customary precision. All his senses were alert to the potential for additional information beyond that openly presented in the missive. He sniffed at the paper, felt the thickness of the stationery, held the correspondence up to the light and scanned every inch with his powerful magnifying lens. Our visitor was mesmerized and held his tongue for some minutes until my colleague addressed him directly: "Mr. Kildare, this is a most interesting communication, and I am grateful to you for bringing it to me. Without doubt, there is some skulduggery at play here. But what were your thoughts when you first read it?" Holmes's eyes were now focused attentively on Kildare as he passed the letter back to me.

"I did not know how to take it, Mr. Holmes. Clearly it contains a threat, both to me and other prominent members of the Society, but beyond that I cannot fathom its rationale or intent. If it is designed merely to promote fear, I can confirm that it has already had the desired effect. There is something in the nature of it which terrifies me and makes me believe that there is genuine menace behind it."

Holmes did not disabuse him of the thought. "Indeed, there is clear intent behind this. I will gladly take your case and have high hopes that we will be able to make some progress very quickly. A few basic facts if you will. Please tell us a little more about the Society and, in particular, the identities of the other members of the 'Paradol Chamber' referred to in the letter? Doctor Watson will note down the salient facts."

Kildare seemed eager to oblige as I reached quickly for a notepad and pen. "Certainly. The Prévost-Paradol Society has over a thousand male members who pay an annual subscription to enable them to enjoy the various events and activities which we organise. In short, these comprise dinners in our building - Wellington House – and talks by authors and journalists who share our liberal views, alongside a wide variety of soirees and get-togethers to honour Lucien-Anatole. The main committee of the Society - which we refer to as our 'Paradol Chamber' - is drawn from the wider membership. Elections take place every six years, the latter being the effective tenure of those chosen by the membership to provide stewardship and oversight of the Society. The elected chamber then selects its own President for the same period of office, a position which I have been privileged to occupy for some six months now. As well as receiving a small stipend, the President is offered the occupancy of an apartment on the top floor of Wellington House and takes charge of the household staff; a concierge, housekeeper, bookkeeper, chef, maid, and personal secretary.

"The other five members of the Paradol Chamber are not paid for their work but can be reimbursed for any expenses they incur in promoting the interests and influence of the Society. The chamber meets in Belgravia four times a year, each meeting taking place on the first day of the month in which they occur – this being March, June, September, and December. The current chamber contains a mixture of talented and capable men who work hard to maintain the profile and reputation of the Society. My own background is in the arts, where I was previously the curator of a major art gallery in Paris. Alongside me, there is Sir Peter Daines, a former British ambassador to France; Claude Ponelle, a journalist from Nice, Nicholas Lamboray, an international banker; Austin Cantwell, an American cattle rancher, and;

Damian Gastineau, an antiquarian book dealer who ordinarily resides in Berlin. I can happily provide you with further information if that would assist you?"

Holmes dismissed the offer with a somewhat nonchalant wave of his hand. "Thank you, Mr. Kildare. For the moment, that is quite sufficient. Now, I suggest you return to Belgravia and ensure that you remain vigilant in the coming hours. I do not believe you to be in any immediate danger but cannot be certain. And for the moment, I would be grateful if you did not mention the letter to any of your chamber colleagues or household staff. Watson and I will call upon you at nine o'clock tomorrow morning, when I will appraise you of our progress. Good morning to you."

Kildare seemed content with Holmes's plan of action and having expressed his gratitude then donned his cape, hat, scarf, and mittens and made for the door. A few minutes later we sat alone in the study. I was finally able to scrutinise the envelope and letter which had prompted our client's visit. The typed note ran as follows:

The Prévost-Paradol Society
Wellington House
Grosvenor Gardens
Belgravia
London

Wednesday, 23ʳᵈ February 1887

To whom it should concern,

You will pay for what you have done. The Paradol Chamber is no sanctuary for your kind - expect swift retribution. And reflect on my name:

47

I start with the sixth, so easy to discern,

Find gold in a table, a symbol to learn.

Derived from the gimel, in temperature and time,

With almost a single, to finish my rhyme.

Vengeance is in my hands,

Anon

"Well, it's certainly cryptic," I said, having read through it three or four times. "What do you make of it?"

Holmes gave me a tell-tale look. "It is most revealing, Watson. The postmark tells us that the letter was posted yesterday in central London. The paper is of a superior quality and matches that of the envelope – stationery from a gentleman's writing set no doubt. And yet the missive is typed, without any obvious errors. So, our writer is either an excellent typist or has made use of someone who is. The timing of the letter is also significant."

"Yes, that I had spotted. From what Kildare told us, the Paradol Chamber will next meet on Tuesday, the first of March. The clear intent is that this 'swift retribution' will occur when the members are next together."

"Indeed. And it seems as if the action is likely to take place at the meeting itself, perpetrated by the writer of this letter; hence the reference to the chamber being 'no sanctuary' and 'vengeance' being in his own hands. The wording also suggests that there is one intended target, although I cannot be certain of that yet. Mark my words, our man intends to act and is brazenly announcing his intention to do so."

"Then he must be one of the chamber members or possibly one of the household staff. An outsider would have no obvious access to the meeting."

"That is my working hypothesis. The fact that he refers specifically to the Paradol Chamber suggests some knowledge of the inner workings of the Society. Perhaps that is why the letter was typed – our man being fearful that his handwriting might be recognised."

"How do you think he intends to act?" I then asked.

Holmes reached for his briar pipe and matches. "That is the crucial question. But I have no doubt he has a canny scheme in mind. The perpetrator sees this as a deadly serious game and has even given us a clue which may help to identify him."

"Yes, that bit I couldn't fathom. The verse meant nothing to me. Why would he risk revealing his name?"

My colleague had succeeded in lighting the pipe and took two or three rapid puffs from it, sending a thick plume of aromatic smoke into the air. "Because, like so many of the colourful characters we encounter in our work, he believes himself to be cleverer than everyone else. That, of course, will be his downfall, his *hubris* or fatal pride."

"Does the verse reveal his name?"

"Possibly. I know what it says, if that is what you're asking. But I suspect it may be something of a smokescreen."

To my frustration, Holmes refused to be drawn further and announced suddenly that he intended to go into town. He took with him my notebook, containing the information I had gleaned from Kildare. I had little doubt that he intended to find out more about the Society and its enigmatic Paradol Chamber.

****

It was just beyond seven o'clock that evening when I heard him return. Mrs. Hudson had already indicated that she had prepared a large shepherd's pie for our supper. I knew she would be relieved that Holmes had returned in good time. Some ten minutes later we were tucking into the delicious dish which the landlady had served, together with a warming glass of cabernet sauvignon.

"A fruitful day, Watson. How did you spend your time?" Holmes asked.

"I attended to a new patient – a Mr. Harold Semper. He has a most interesting case of cretinism."

"That would explain the faint smell of iodine I detect about you. I could not be certain that you had used it to treat someone with thyroid problems - for I know that iodine has many medical uses - but if pushed, that would have been my supposition."

"And your progress?"

"A most productive day. I made a few enquiries relating to the Bassey-Fisher abduction case, but also found time to visit the British Library and countless government buildings to gather relevant information on the Kildare mystery. I now have a much clearer understanding of the nature of the Prévost-Paradol Society, and I have to say it is not what I expected."

I looked across at him, my fork balanced before me with a steaming mouthful of creamy mashed potato. "Really? You surprise me. I imagined it to be a pukka gentlemen's club."

"No. In fact, it has run into difficulties in recent years and there have even been rumours of fraud among earlier members of the Paradol Chamber. While the Society was set up to honour the intellect and democratic ideals of Lucien-Anatole Prévost-Paradol, it has descended into something of a Hellfire Club. Members are carefully vetted before they are permitted to join and then pay a sizeable fee each year to partake of an annual programme of events largely designed to cater for their salacious desires and appetites. Still, perhaps they see Lucien-Anatole's early history as the perfect metaphor for their dubious activities. He was, after all, conceived as a result of an irregular liaison between the renowned opera singer Lucinde Paradol and the writer Léon Halévy."

I could not help but smile at my friend's pejorative stance but let the matter rest. "So, given the nature of the Society, I imagine that elevation to the Paradol Chamber is seen by many to be a coveted position. Its members effectively control both the Society's finances and its social activities."

"You are not wrong. Even being shortlisted for consideration as an election candidate is perceived to be a cloak and dagger affair. Large sums of money can often change hands to secure enough votes to be in the running. And elevation to the post of President is viewed as a similarly contentious affair."

"Then are we to trust Mr. Kildare?"

"It is hard to say. One or two of my well-placed contacts view him as a force for good. He has vowed to improve the governance and status of the Society and has already set about making some key changes. On his appointment six months back, he let all the existing employees go and recruited a new household staff. While he received the backing of the Paradol Chamber, there was some disquiet about the decision."

"Perhaps that is what lies behind the threatening letter – possibly one of the disgruntled employees?"

It seemed a reasonable assumption, yet Holmes frowned at the thought. "I'm inclined to believe otherwise, Watson. These are dark waters and I'm convinced that the motivation runs much deeper."

"What of the other chamber members, did you manage to find out anything about them?" I then asked.

Holmes had clearly eaten as much of the shepherd's pie as he was inclined to, a little less than a third of the generous serving that Mrs. Hudson had given him. He placed his knife and fork on the plate and gently slid it away from him. "A mixed bunch. Sir Peter Daines enjoyed a meteoric career, brought to an abrupt halt when he seduced the then wife of the French Foreign Minister. By all accounts he is something of a serial philanderer. Claude Ponelle, the journalist, writes for a scurrilous French newspaper and is often challenged in the courts for defaming high-profile politicians. Nicholas Lamboray, whom Kildare described somewhat euphemistically as 'an international banker', appears to have made his money through several fraudulent investment schemes, most notably providing the funding for Sarah Emily Howe's infamous Ladies' Deposit Company in Boston, which swindled 1,200 unmarried women out of their savings seven or eight years ago.

"The American, Austin Cantwell, has a similarly inglorious background. He used strong-arm tactics to force several Texan ranch owners off their lands, which he then purchased for his own cattle empire, making himself quite a fortune. And lastly, we have Damian Gastineau, the antiquarian book dealer. In short, he deals only in one specific, and highly lucrative, trade – that of rare pornographic texts. The Berlin apartment building he owns is rumoured to be one of the most expensive private properties in the city."

I was staggered by the revelations. "A veritable bunch of charlatans then. And what of Anthony Kildare? Does he have a dubious past as well?"

Holmes grinned. "Now there is the biggest conundrum. He seems to have led an exemplary life. A dedicated and talented professional who was well regarded in the art world. As well as making himself and his clients rich through the sale of their art treasures, he has been something of a visionary philanthropist, donating vast sums to alleviate street poverty in Paris."

"Then he really does appear to be a force for good. So why would the others have rallied to support his presidential candidacy?"

He drained what remained of his red wine and beamed. "I said that he *seems* to have led an exemplary life. It does not follow that he has been virtuous in all respects. The art world is one of the most criminally corrupt trades in existence. Fakes and forgeries abound. Fortunes are made and lost. Art, like beauty, is indeed in the eye of the beholder. It is my contention that Mr. Kildare has occasionally dabbled in art fraud. The only difference between him and the other members of the Paradol Chamber is that he has never been caught or exposed for his nefarious activities."

****

The following morning, we set off in good time to reach Wellington House for our nine o'clock appointment. A thick fog had descended upon the capital and our cabbie drove both slowly and cautiously given the limited visibility. The temperature was unseasonably cold, and the fog deposited a fine layer of mist on our thick overcoats. Holmes seemed not to notice the inclement conditions, but I shivered throughout most of the journey.

Wellington House was a grand three storey building set within a half-acre plot. Two sizeable columns framed the main entrance, the solid double doors of which led us into an ornate and heavily marbled foyer. As we entered, we were greeted by a uniformed concierge. "Good morning, gentlemen. You must be Mr. Sherlock Holmes and Dr. Watson. Mr. Kildare is expecting you but has been somewhat delayed by the unfortunate incident in the boardroom. It's a terrible business, to be sure. The doctor is still here."

Holmes addressed the concierge very directly. "What was the nature of this *unfortunate incident*? Has someone been hurt?"

"It's Mrs. Throckmorton, the housekeeper. Her body was found in the boardroom earlier this morning. She must have suffered some sort of fit or heart attack. Mr. Kildare says that her body has been there all night, as it was her final job yesterday to clean and polish the silverware in the boardroom. She retained a key to a door at the back of the house, so we all assumed she had finished the polishing and had gone home for the evening."

"I see. Would it be possible for us to see the body? It may have some bearing on our investigations."

The concierge had clearly not been told about the nature of our enquiries and looked bewildered as to why we would want to view the corpse. He looked towards me for some reassurance or explanation. I responded accordingly: "It wouldn't hurt to have a second opinion. I'm sure the other doctor would not mind."

The concierge pointed us towards the central staircase and invited us to ascend to the third floor. The landing on which we emerged was spacious and exquisitely decorated. A glittering chandelier hung above our heads and all along the walls to the left and right were large oil paintings and the occasional plinth, on which were sat bronze heads and well executed plaster cast busts. I could see that Holmes was surveying each in turn.

We were greeted by a fraught-looking Anthony Kildare. "Gentlemen, my sincere apologies. I'm sure that Mr. Hargreaves, the concierge, has alerted you to the sad demise of our housekeeper. The doctor we called is still with the body and I hope that he will attend to all of the formalities required." His manner was considerably more congenial than it had been the previous day. "Would you like to step this way? I will take you along to my office."

Holmes was in no mood to be moved on. "I would be most obliged if you would allow Dr. Watson and I to see the body. I take it that the boardroom is this way, to the left? He turned and began to walk along the corridor without waiting for an answer.

Kildare looked momentarily confused and then began to trot along behind him. "Of course, Mr. Holmes. But I don't see how this is likely to be relevant to your enquiries. Mrs. Throckmorton was not in the best of health. It was only recently that she managed to overcome a bad case of influenza."

I followed Kildare, and at the end of the corridor we were faced with two heavy oak doors which led into the Society's boardroom. The door to the left was open, revealing a small rectangular room, down the centre of which sat a large oval table and solid refectory chairs. Along both walls were plaques of various kinds, some listing what I imagined to be current or previous members of the Paradol Chamber. At the far end were some ornate glass cabinets containing a large collection of silver trophies and plates.

While the room had no windows, it was lit by a sizeable glass skylight set high above. I could already see the doctor squatting on the floor beside the body of the late Mrs. Throckmorton, his medical bag resting by his right knee. Holmes gently swung the right-hand door open to its fullest extent and stepped cautiously into the room. He then invited me to do the same but asked Kildare to remain in the corridor.

"Doctor Trent," said the man facing us. "Can I help you, gentlemen?"

"Sherlock Holmes," replied my colleague. "And this is Dr. Watson. We are currently investigating a threat that has been made to prominent members of the Prévost-Paradol Society. I would welcome your opinion as to the nature of the housekeeper's death and whether it was the result of natural causes."

Trent smiled uncomfortably. "Are you from Scotland Yard?"

"No, I am a private detective, and my associate is a medical man just like yourself."

The man looked from Holmes towards me and smiled once more. "It is a pleasure to meet you, Dr. Watson. Your arrival is very timely, for I would very much welcome your professional view alongside my own. There are some complications which I had not anticipated."

I stepped over to join Dr. Trent at the head of the body. The cadaver was lying face down, the head twisted slightly to the right. And the housekeeper's arms were stretched out before her in the direction of the door. Holmes seemed content for me to confer with the good doctor, which I began to do in hushed tones, aware that Mr. Kildare was at that time pacing up and down in the corridor behind us. In his inimitable fashion, Holmes then began to survey every inch of the room with his magnifying glass, at one stage lying on the floor and looking up at the skylight. It was a good ten minutes before he re-joined us at the entrance to the boardroom, stepping out briefly to invite Kildare to enter.

Our client looked none too pleased as he took his place beside Holmes. The detective then directed his attention towards him: "Who was it that found the body?"

"My personal assistant, Peregrine Cattermole. He arrived at work at eight o'clock this morning and was unable to locate Mrs. Throckmorton. Ordinarily, our housekeeper spends most of her time on the ground floor, overseeing the work of the maid, chef, and bookkeeper. When Mr. Hargreaves confirmed that he had not seen anything of her, Peregrine came up to the third floor and found the poor woman as you see her now."

"Were the doors to the boardroom locked when Mr. Cattermole arrived?" asked Holmes.

"No, that I can say with certainty, for there are only two sets of keys to the boardroom. I retain one, while Mrs. Throckmorton held the main set. Each door must be unlocked from the outside to gain entry. You can see that both of her keys are still in the outside locks, so she could not have locked the doors from the inside."

A troubled look passed briefly over Holmes's face. "I see. And did no one query Mrs. Throckmorton's absence prior to that? Presumably, she lived somewhere close by and had a family who might have been troubled by her non-appearance yesterday evening?"

"No," replied Kildare once again. "She lived alone, with only a handful of cats for company. It was one of the reasons I employed her. She had no other distractions or responsibilities and was dedicated to the job. She was always prepared to work late or start earlier than normal and was a first-rate housekeeper. Nothing much escaped her attention."

I felt his closing remark was delivered with just a hint of cynicism but did not challenge him. Holmes then said: "Thank you, Mr. Kildare. I don't have any further questions at this stage. I'm sure that this is a straightforward case of death by natural causes but will ask my medical colleagues here to brief me on what they have found before the body is removed. Is it possible that Watson and I could join you in your office in a short while?"

Kildare voiced no objection, adding only that, "my office and apartment are to the right of the main staircase. I'll wait for you there. I will also arrange for you to meet Peregrine Cattermole. His office is on the second floor. Should I ask him to join us, or would you prefer to meet him down below?"

Holmes was most direct. "I would much prefer to speak to Mr. Cattermole alone. And a little later it would be useful to speak to the other members of the household staff."

"As you wish," replied our client, turning and heading off along the corridor.

It was as if all three of us knew instinctively to wait until Kildare had departed before resuming our discussions. A moment later Holmes confided in Dr. Trent. "I am sorry for my little charade, Doctor. But at this stage, I am not sure what to make of our Mr. Kildare. Now, I believe you are about to tell me that Mrs. Throckmorton died as a result of a pulmonary edema – the fluid accumulation in her lungs making it difficult for her to breath and resulting in respiratory failure."

Dr. Trent looked astonished. I too was intrigued to know how he could have made the diagnosis without examining the body, but it was Trent who spoke first. "How did you know that? While Dr. Watson and I were conferring, you did nothing but amble around the room with that eyeglass of yours." His tone then became a little more antagonistic: "But then I wonder if you already knew what to expect?"

I felt I had to step in to protect Holmes's reputation, if not his safety, for Dr. Trent's easy-going countenance had given way to something approaching hostility. "Doctor. Please do not be alarmed by my friend's pronouncement. He has a rare set of talents and an ability to observe things that others so easily overlook. I'm sure that he will happily explain himself."

Holmes took my cue and sought to reassure Trent. "My good man, I apologise for unnerving you. Watson will tell you that I have a terrible habit of announcing conclusions without explaining the facts, reasoning, or logic behind them. On entering the room, I looked first towards the body. The position and outstretched arms were highly suggestive as if the housekeeper were attempting to make for the doors and had fallen forwards. A trolley containing all the paraphernalia for cleaning and polishing the boardroom's silverware still sits at the far end of the room, obscured from where we are now by the position of the table. A duster and a tin of silver polish lie discarded on the floor. Clearly, she had been working before something had induced her to try and leave the room.

"The frothy pink sputum, visible at the sides of the mouth, shows that she coughed up some blood before dying. The pale skin and bloodshot eyes lend further weight to the idea that respiratory failure was the cause of death. Yet this was not the result of heart failure, for the pulmonary edema was triggered by a chemical agent."

Dr. Trent interjected: "Are you saying the woman was poisoned? Watson and I had already identified that that was one of the possibilities, but agreed that a *post mortem* would be needed to prove it."

"Yes. To be precise, she was asphyxiated by phosphine gas. You will know that the ordinarily odourless respiratory poison starves the body of oxygen and causes the lungs to fill with fluid. On the far wall, to the right of the boardroom is a metal handle which extends upwards and enables a section of the skylight to be opened for ventilation purposes. This has been opened and then closed again recently. A small amount of grit and debris - which most likely accumulated on the glass of the skylight during the winter months – has fallen to the floor. It is my contention that the gas was pumped into the room through the skylight and, being heavier than air, descended slowly to the floor, seeping into Mrs. Throckmorton's lungs. Time has allowed the remaining gas to disperse, but close to the floor I detected a faint whiff of rotting fish – clear evidence of the crudely manufactured phosphine gas which contained one or more trace contaminants."

"Truly remarkable!" cried Trent. "Then it's a case of murder."

Holmes nodded. "The killer most likely believed that the crime would not be detected. We know that Mrs. Throckmorton had not been well recently, and you said yourselves that poisoning was only one of the possibilities you had identified. It would be easy to conclude that this was a natural death given the women's age and health."

Dr. Trent still looked stunned by the revelation. "But why would the culprit go to such extraordinary lengths to kill this poor woman? There would have been far easier ways to despatch her."

Holmes looked thoughtfully towards the body. "I fear it was but a prelude to a much more elaborate scheme. Having tested the efficacy of his method, I believe our killer will attempt to strike again."

I knew he was alluding to the upcoming meeting of the Paradol Chamber, but he seemed reluctant to say any more. I then voiced a practical consideration. "Should we not inform Scotland Yard about the murder?"

"I have reflected on that but believe it might harm our chances of catching the killer. It is in our interests for him to believe he has carried out an undetected homicide. That way, he will carry on and we will have every chance of acting to prevent further death. I will, of course, be guided by you, Dr. Trent. This is very much in your professional domain."

The appeal to the doctor's professional integrity was a clever move. Trent thought for a few seconds and then announced he was comfortable to comply with such a plan. "I will note all of the findings I had made prior to your arrival and record that the death is, at this stage, *unexplained*. That will give me sufficient leeway to carry out the *post mortem* where evidence of the poisoning should be evident. At that stage, I will alert Scotland Yard."

"Rest assured. If you have any difficulties in dealing with the police, Watson and I will be pleased to step in and assist. We have built a good rapport with many of the senior detectives in the metropolitan force and can use that to our advantage."

"That is kind of you, Mr. Holmes. I will arrange for the body to be taken from here to my surgery in Wilton Street and will be sure to share the findings of the autopsy with you. Dr. Watson has given me his card."

We left Trent at that point and set off down the corridor towards the landing of the third floor. On three occasions, Holmes stopped and paid particular attention to some of the paintings lining the wall. On the final stop, he extracted his magnifying glass from an inside pocket and examined the oil painting at close quarters. "Extraordinary!" he whispered.

"What is extraordinary?" I asked quietly.

"Three of these paintings are extremely rare and undoubtedly valuable. And yet they hang here with little protection."

"Yes, I suppose that is surprising."

He looked at me with some disgruntlement. "No, that is not the extraordinary factor. The surprising fact is that they are genuine." Without elaborating, he moved on, leaving me to pick up the pace as he strode purposefully towards Kildare's office and private quarters.

Our client was at work within a light, spacious and sumptuously decorated office. The walls were decorated with more oil paintings and several framed certificates. From the window behind Kildare's large, leather-clad desk he had an incredible view out over the mansions and well-appointed gardens of Belgravia. He beckoned for us to take the two seats which sat in front of the desk and then gestured towards a drinks cabinet on his left. "May I offer you some refreshments?"

Holmes declined, but reached for his pipe and matches. I felt it only courteous to accept the offer and asked for a small sherry. As Kildare poured the drink, my friend lit the pipe and sat back in his chair looking around the room. "Now, that is curious, Mr. Kildare. I had understood you to be a man of the arts, and yet it seems your talents extend into other fields as well."

Kildare followed Holmes's gaze, which was now centred on a framed certificate on the wall to the man's left. "Aha! I see that your reputation as a detective is well deserved. Few people know that before I started my career in the art world, I had studied at the Ecole Supérieure de Commerce de Paris. That was where I developed my deep affection for the city. While I was born in Cambridge, I see Paris as my adopted home and retain an apartment there which I return to whenever I can. Now, how is your investigation progressing?"

"Very well," replied Holmes. "I am convinced that the threatening letter is genuine and believe that some attempt will be made on the lives of those attending the Paradol Chamber meeting next week."

"I see. And do you have any plans to thwart this attempt?"

"Yes. With your permission, Watson and I would like to sit in on the meeting, fully armed. That way, we can respond to any threat which may present itself."

"Excellent!" replied Kildare. His face lit up with undisguised joy. "And do you have any idea who might be behind all of this?"

"I have my suspicions but need to confirm a few more details. I do believe it to be the work of someone within the Society but would prefer to say no more at this stage. Could I confirm that you have not told anyone else about the contents of the letter?"

"You can take that as read. I briefed all the staff about your visit today but explained only that you were helping me with an investigation into some irregularities regarding the finances of the Society. They have been told to answer any questions you may wish to put to them."

"That is most helpful. I would suggest that Watson interviews all the staff on the ground floor – whom I believe to be the concierge, chef, bookkeeper, and maid. At the same time, I will speak to Mr. Cattermole on the second floor. Does he keep records relating to the membership of the Society and minutes of your chamber meetings?"

Kildare confirmed that this was indeed the case. Holmes then had one final request. "Would it be possible for us to meet the other five members of the Paradol Chamber in advance of the meeting?"

The request seemed to surprise Kildare. "I have no objection, but in practical terms the only opportunity you will have to do so will be tomorrow evening. On Saturday, we are hosting one of our regular soirees with around a hundred attendees. The drinks reception begins at six-thirty and after an hour or so the members are free to choose how they spend their time. We have four different rooms which offer our gentlemen various forms of entertainment according to their particular interests. I would be pleased to arrange for you to attend the drinks reception. That would not breach any of the Society's accepted rules."

It was all I could do not to laugh at Kildare's euphemistic description of the event. He was clearly trying to maintain the charade that the Prévost-Paradol Society was a respectable gentlemen's club. Holmes also remained straight-faced and merely thanked our client, saying that we would be pleased to depart at seven-thirty.

At that point, I placed my sherry glass down on Kildare's desk and rose from the chair, believing our meeting with the man to be at an end and reflecting on the sorts of questions I might wish to ask of the staff on the ground floor. To my surprise, Holmes remained seated and proceeded to ask Kildare a rather obscure question: "I noticed along the corridor that you have three exceptional oil paintings. If I am not mistaken, there is a painting by Paul Cézanne and two by Pierre-Auguste Renoir. I am curious to know how you came by them and whether you allow your maid to dust them regularly."

Kildare took a second or two to answer, no doubt curious as to what Holmes was driving at. "The paintings are on loan to us and belong to two of the members of the Paradol Chamber. The Cézanne is owned by Damian Gastineau, while the two paintings by Renoir are the property of Austin Cantwell. They have agreed that the paintings will be displayed until they cease to be members of the chamber. As to dusting, I wouldn't let the maid anywhere near them. They are far too valuable."

Holmes chuckled and rose from his chair. "That is perfectly understandable. Now, to work, Watson. I will speak with Mr. Cattermole, while you head to the ground floor. Thank you again for your time, Mr. Kildare. It has been most useful. I dare say we will need no more than a couple of hours to conclude our business here today."

We shook hands with the man and made our way back down the corridor. At the top of the stairs, Holmes paused and whispered to me. "It would be best not to share our thoughts at this stage, for I am sure that our conversation will be overheard. Could I suggest that we confer on the way back to Baker Street when we have finished here today?"

I had no objection and left Holmes when we reached the second floor. At ground level, I began my own interviews with a visit to the concierge, taking careful notes of what I considered to be useful and relevant facts. Bill Hargreaves was an affable fellow, with a solid military background. He was concerned to know what the doctor had concluded about the death of Mrs. Throckmorton. I did not wish to reveal any of the details and stated only that the examination had proved inconclusive and a *post mortem* would be needed.

Asked about his work, Hargreaves said that he adopted a 'no nonsense' approach to his dealings with both the household staff and members of the Society. Generally, he found them to be pleasant enough, although he had reservations about the banker, Nicholas Lamboray, whom he described as 'a jumped-up, arrogant, and manipulative man, who thinks he's better than everyone else'. He believed Anthony Kildare to be a capable figurehead but admitted that on a day-to-day basis he saw little of him. Similarly, he rarely encountered Peregrine Cattermole, who apparently spent most of his working hours shut in his office and always left at five o'clock each afternoon. The only exception to this routine was on the first of September, the previous year, when he had been required to take the minutes of his first Paradol Chamber meeting.

My final question to Hargreaves had been something of a throwaway remark but elicited a most curious response. I said I was aware of the colourful nature of some of the

Society's social events and wondered if he had ever seen anything which had surprised him. He admitted that as a long-serving sergeant in the British Army he had encountered his fair share of lewd behaviour and bawdy entertainment. That did not concern him. But what he did find odd, was the nature of the supplies which Mr. Kildare ordered in on a regular basis and required him to carry up to the third floor. In recent months, this had included paints, oils, turpentine, and sealed containers of chemicals with strange sounding names. On one occasion, he had asked Peregrine Cattermole about the deliveries, and the personal secretary said that he understood Kildare to be preparing for the decoration of his apartment. And yet, to date, no decorators had been employed to carry out the work.

My discussions with Pierre Sabatini, the resident French chef, revealed little of interest. He had a full workload, preparing all the food required in the household - morning, noon, and night. For the Society's events he employed additional kitchen and serving staff as required. He rarely saw the other members of staff and avoided contact with the members of the Society whom he described, rather cuttingly, as "spoilt rich men".

Tilly Norton, the housemaid, was also able to provide little by way of information. Like the other members of staff, she did not live in, and her hours of work were strictly "eight 'til four". She had been close to Mrs. Throckmorton, who had directed all her work, and seemed tearful at the mere mention of the housekeeper's name. When first employed, she had occasionally helped as a waitress at some of the Society's dinners but had asked the housekeeper if she might be relieved of such duties as she found the attentions of some of the members to be "unsavoury". I did not press her further on the matter.

My final interview was with Stanley Dunn, the Society's bookkeeper. He was a skinny, pale-faced man in his mid-thirties, with unkempt sandy hair and a dishevelled appearance. There was something likeable about the fellow and I found him to be open and forthcoming in his response to my questions. He revealed that he had found clear evidence of widespread fraud and irregularities in the Society's accounts stretching back for several years. Previous members of the Paradol Chamber had used their position to claim expenses they had not incurred and had authorised illicit payments for a variety of dubious activities. Mr. Kildare had employed Dunn on the understanding that all this activity was to stop, and the financial probity of the Society should be an integral part of its continued operation. The President had been wholly supportive of Dunn's work to strengthen all the governance arrangements within the organisation.

Like the concierge, Dunn asked about the doctor's conclusions regarding the death of Mrs. Throckmorton. I responded as I had with Bill Hargreaves. He said he respected the housekeeper, who had always worked to the most exacting standards, keeping Wellington House in good shape. He had been about to leave his office the previous evening at the time when Mr. Kildare came down to ask for the silverware in the boardroom to be polished. The door to Mrs. Throckmorton's small office had been ajar and he was able to hear fragments of their conversation. The housekeeper had said something about 'painting Mr. Cattermole's office' which seemed to agitate Kildare. He then asked Mrs. Throckmorton if she could ensure that the silverware in the boardroom was polished before the light faded. Dunn heard her readily agree to the task, but she had asked politely whether it could wait until the morning. Kildare had apparently insisted that it must be done there and then. The bookkeeper had been surprised by this as it was a task usually undertaken by the housemaid.

With little more to be gleaned from the staff, I made my way back to the entrance and spent a few minutes chatting to Bill Hargreaves about my own military past. Holmes then descended the stairwell with the broadest of grins and a distinct skip in his step. I could already tell that his afternoon had borne fruit. We thanked Hargreaves and said our goodbyes, explaining that we would be attending the drinks reception the following evening so would see him again then.

On the thoroughfare outside of the drive to Wellington House we were able to hail a cab within five minutes. It was just as well, for the fog had lifted giving way to a light shower and the temperature seemed not to have risen at all. The hansom carried us slowly but steadily back to Baker Street, and for whole of the journey Holmes was mired in thought.

****

It took me some time to warm through, sat before the fire in 221B with my hands outstretched. Having arrived back, Holmes busied himself responding to a couple of telegrams he had received that afternoon from a lawyer in Brussels, a client in a kidnapping case which had been brought to a successful conclusion two weeks earlier. When he finally took to his seat, he was eager to hear what I had discovered from my interviews with the staff. "Do not overlook any details, my good friend. This case is becoming clearer by the minute, yet a few crucial details still elude me." I was gratified to hear him say this, for I felt no nearer to understanding what lay behind the case than I did the previous day.

I spent the next twenty minutes running through the notes I had made, with Holmes interjecting once or twice on some small points of detail. When I had finished, he congratulated me wholeheartedly. "You've done a splendid job, Watson. Alongside my own efforts this afternoon, I believe we have now laid bare all the pertinent facts behind this dastardly scheme. And not before time. Had we not done so, there would surely have been a further eight deaths next Tuesday."

I was taken aback. "Eight deaths, you say? But there are only six members of the Paradol Chamber."

"You are forgetting Peregrine Cattermole, the private secretary, who will be taking notes."

"Accepted, although that still only accounts for seven."

"It must be clear to you now that our mystery assailant is Anthony Kildare. He has it in mind to murder Cattermole and all five of his chamber colleagues. In addition, he believes he has hoodwinked you and I in agreeing to attend the meeting so that we also fall prey to his deadly poison."

I was shaken by the disclosure and the thought that our short-sighted client was behind such an elaborate plot. "But why come to us in the first place? Surely it would have suited his purpose better if he'd been able to carry out his plan without the complication of our involvement?"

Holmes tapped the ash from his pipe into the hearth and began to refill the bowl with some rough shag tobacco. "*Hubris*. I said so earlier. Kildare believes himself to be a master manipulator. I believe that my work has, in the past, caused him some material hardship. Some years back, I was commissioned by the Swiss government to intercept a shipment of paintings stolen from a gallery in Zurich. While I managed to successfully locate and return the missing masterpieces, I was never able to identify the orchestrator of the audacious heist. I now believe that person was Kildare and can imagine that he would take great delight in laying before me a case which would ultimately lead me to my death.

"It was clear from the outset that Kildare knew of my work and reputation. When he came to Baker Street, he knew immediately that I was the detective and not your good self. He claimed his personal secretary had told him about me, yet in my discussions this afternoon it soon became clear that Peregrine Cattermole had no idea who I was. And when I quizzed Kildare about his certificate from the Ecole Supérieure de Commerce de Paris he admitted that my *reputation as a detective was well deserved.*"

"I can see all of that," I replied, "but what of the cryptic letter?"

He smirked as he retrieved the letter from the inside pocket of his jacket and passed it across to me. "We will come to that in due course. Let us begin by establishing Kildare's basic motivation in becoming President of the Prévost-Paradol Society. Does it surprise you to learn that he has engineered everything thus far for financial gain?"

On this I felt I had to challenge my friend. "It would. You said yourself that your contacts had described Kildare as a force for good in his stewardship of the Society. He has made changes to improve its governance and the bookkeeper was adamant that the President is committed to maintaining the financial integrity of the organisation."

"Indeed, he may be. But the financial gain was to come not from the Society, but from two members of the Paradol Chamber. While I was with Cattermole, I asked to see the membership records of the Society and other relevant documentation. This revealed that while Sir Peter Daines and Claude Ponelle have been long-standing members, Kildare, Lamboray, Gastineau and Cantwell all joined at the same time – only eight months ago. In fact, when asked, Cattermole confirmed that Lamboray and Kildare have been friends for some years, and he understood Gastineau and Cantwell to be clients of the international banker. Clearly, the four men conspired to elevate themselves to the Paradol Chamber, using their own wealth to buy votes from other members. Having done so, they agreed that Kildare would take on the role of President. Since that time, they have voted as a bloc on all key decisions. While Daines and Ponelle have voiced some dissension, they cannot outvote the others."

He paused to take a further draw on his briar pipe, then continued. "Now we come to the crux of the deception. Kildare managed to persuade his associates that all the existing staff should be replaced. They agreed to back the decision, although Daines and Ponelle voted against it. He did this firstly - as any new leader might - to allow him to introduce reforms that would improve the reputation and standing of the organisation. With what he had in mind, the last thing he wanted was the unnecessary scrutiny of anyone on the outside. But the changes also enabled him to employ a new member of staff, in a post that had not previously existed. Namely, that of Peregrine Cattermole, the personal secretary. The Paradol Chamber may believe him to be a suitably experienced administrator, but I can assure you he is not. The minutes he took at his first, and only, chamber meeting last year are appalling, and it is quite clear that he is no typist."

I interposed, confused as to where this was leading. "Then why would Kildare employ such a fellow? The other staff seem very competent in comparison."

Holmes seemed to relish the challenge. "Cattermole was recruited for one specific purpose. When I entered his office today, my olfactory senses were stimulated by several distinct odours; the faint smell of oil paint, a hint of turpentine and the aroma of linseed oil. While he had tried to wash his hands of all traces, he still had tiny spots of oil paint on both his hands and shirt cuffs. The man is no secretary, but an artist of the highest calibre."

I could see how this tied in with one of my earlier discussions. "That would explain the odd delivery of supplies that Hargreaves, the concierge, referred to."

"It does. So at the heart of this is an attempt to commit art forgery. I believe that Lamboray convinced his banking clients Gastineau and Cantwell to lend the Society three extremely valuable paintings. No doubt they are insured, and through their dealings with Kildare, both men are likely to believe him to be the perfect caretaker for their masterpieces. My examination of all three works showed that they had been removed from the wall and put back frequently, hence my question to Kildare about whether the maid had been allowed to polish the paintings. Piecing together all that we now know, it is clear that Cattermole has been commissioned to create forgeries of the paintings. And once these fakes have been hung on the wall of the third floor, Kildare will be able to sell the genuine canvasses through his network of contacts across Europe."

"Incredible! And yet, you believe he also plans to outwit both Lamboray and Cattermole by poisoning them with the others?"

"Exactly. As neat a scheme as could ever be devised. And the unfortunate Mrs. Throckmorton presented Kildare with the perfect opportunity to test his deadly phosphine. I think the bookkeeper was mistaken when he said he heard the housekeeper refer to 'painting Mr. Cattermole's office'. I believe that what she really told Kildare was that she had seen *a painting in Mr. Cattermole's office*. This set him on edge, for he realised that the scheme could easily unravel with what she had witnessed. Knowing that Cattermole had left work at five o'clock, and no one else was likely to be around on the third floor besides himself, Kildare hastily asked Mrs. Throckmorton to collect her trolley and go up to the boardroom to polish the silverware. While she collected her things, he made his way to the room and opened the skylight. He then re-locked the double doors and waited for her to appear. When she had unlocked both doors using her own set of keys and had gone into the boardroom, he locked her in from the outside. He then made his way onto the roof through a door in his office and surreptitiously pumped the phosphine gas in through the skylight. Later he returned to unlock the doors to the study but did not open them. He knew that the calculated quantity of gas he had released would be largely dispersed overnight, leaving little trace in the morning."

The genius of this twisted execution had to be acknowledged, but my thoughts turned quickly to the excruciating death the poor woman must have faced. It then occurred to me: "How did you know Kildare had a door leading to the roof?"

"I didn't at first. But realised there had to be some way of getting on to the roof to clean and maintain the skylight. When we were in Kildare's office, I observed a small doorway in the far corner on which was a printed sign reading 'Maintenance Only'."

"Very neat," I acknowledged, "but how was he able to procure the gas? I recollect that the chemist Paul Thénard was able to generate phosphine from calcium phosphide in the 1840s, but it is by no means an easy process. To produce enough gas would require some industry. I also seem to remember that the gas can be spontaneously flammable in air."

"You are quite correct. But enough gas could be produced by simply heating phosphorus in an aqueous solution of potash – Philippe Gengembre did so as early as 1783. I am certain that Kildare has the chemical and technical knowledge to overcome the production challenges. The certificate on his wall showed that his studies in Paris were in *Engineering and Natural Sciences.* And while he sought to distract my attention away from it, with the talk of his affection for the city, I already knew from my research that he spent some time working as an industrial chemist before entering the art world. Some of the odd supplies carried up to the third floor by the concierge were almost certainly the strangely named chemicals he needed to manufacture the gas. If he has already installed some sort of gas pumping system near the skylight, he is certain to have a make-shift laboratory set up on the roof."

It was a terrifying thought, and I realised all too clearly how dangerous our adversary was. But I still did not understand how the cryptic letter fitted into the plan and unfolded it once more to try and make sense of it.

"That was the easiest part of all," admitted Holmes, "and my first clue that Kildare was behind this himself. The missive is clumsy and seeks to implicate Cattermole. The secretary has a typewriter in his office which was the machine used to produce the letter. The way that the type stamps out the letter 'd' is quite distinct and can be seen on other records and correspondence. Kildare typed the letter himself and is considerably more accurate than his secretary. The stationery is the same as that used by Cattermole."

"But you still haven't explained the coded name," I said with growing anticipation.

"The rhyme was simplicity itself. *I start with the sixth, so easy to discern* gives us 'F' – the sixth letter of the alphabet.

Find gold in a table, a symbol to learn is a little more obscure, but you will recollect that Dmitri Mendeleev produced his 'Periodic Table' in 1871, arranging all the chemical elements by their atomic mass and assigning each a symbol. In his table, gold is symbolised as 'Au'. *Derived from the gimel, in temperature and time* requires us to consider the ancient Semitic languages, in which *gimel* is represented by the letter 'C' or 'G', for both have the same derivation. Yet as the rhyme refers also to *temperature and time,* we can assume that the fourth letter is 'C', as in 'centigrade' and 'century'. *With almost a single, to finish my rhyme* is simple wordplay. A single would be 'One', *almost one* could be interpreted as 'On'. So, taken together, our name reads *Faucon.*"

"The French for *Falcon*! Thus pointing us in the direction of *Peregrine* Cattermole!"

"Indeed. And with the progress we have made today, I believe a treat would be in order. What say you to supper at the *Criterion*?"

****

I arose somewhat later than planned on the Saturday morning to find Holmes already breakfasted and in a jubilant mood. Bright sunlight was already streaming into the apartment and the weather looked as if it had improved considerably. I sat down at the table with a warming cup of tea and two thick slices of toast.

"Good morning, Watson! Any later, and half the day would have been gone! This evening will be essential in strengthening the case against Kildare. I have but one hour to ensure that the trap is sprung. And I will need you to be at your most gregarious in talking to the members of the

Paradol Chamber and thus distracting them from my activities."

"Then your request to meet the chamber members was no more than a ruse?"

"Precisely. Our case hinges on the physical evidence of the forged paintings and confirmation of the existence of the phosphine gas. At present, both are hypothetical. I have conjectured that they exist but have not seen them first-hand. So, while you are at your most genial this evening, I plan to slip out and visit both Cattermole's office and the rooftop laboratory. If I fail in the task, our case will be severely weakened."

The challenge facing us occupied my thoughts throughout the morning. In contrast, Holmes seemed unperturbed and decidedly resolute, brushing down his expensively tailored dinner jacket and seeking out his best top hat in readiness for the evening reception.

Around two o'clock, Mrs. Hudson knocked on our door and announced the arrival of a telegram. It was from Dr. Trent and summarised the results of his autopsy, saying simply *'PM completed – clear evidence of gas poisoning – SY informed'*. Holmes was not surprised but looked momentarily irritated. "I had hoped that Trent might be a little tardy in undertaking the *post mortem*," he declared reaching for his Ulster and hat. "I will have to square this with Inspector Lestrade at the Yard, otherwise we are likely to have half the Metropolitan force running amok on the corridors of Wellington House. The timing could not have been worse."

So saying, he set off down the stairs promising to be back in good time for our journey to Belgravia. For the rest of the afternoon, I did my best to catch up on some neglected paperwork from my medical practice and was relieved to hear my colleague's familiar footfall on the stairs a little before five-thirty.

"Success, I believe, Watson. Lestrade was not pleased but has agreed that his men will not take any action at present in investigating the death of Mrs. Throckmorton. I had to reveal to him the full facts of what we have discovered. He seemed highly sceptical about the whole affair but wished us well in our exploits this evening. However, he has insisted on a heavy police presence next Tuesday when we bring Kildare to justice. I have still to arrange the choreography of that with him."

"Then we are all set," I replied, no less nervous than I had been five minutes earlier.

It seemed fitting that we should book a four-wheeler to transport us to Belgravia. We followed two other carriages along the short drive to Wellington House and finally stepped into the foyer of the building at around six-twenty. Bill Hargreaves gave us an effusive welcome, shaking our hands with some vigour and pointing us towards a long corridor which led to the Society's palatial ball room.

It was certainly a lavish affair, with canapés, choice cut meats and the very freshest seafood. I had never seen so many fine Champagnes assembled on one table, and the pretty waitresses who were endlessly circling the oval-shaped hall were dispensing it with little regard for the costs involved.

I heard Anthony Kildare before I chanced to see him in action - his loud, clipped diction cutting through the ceaseless babble of voices in the high-ceiled room. He was wearing a long, crimson dinner jacket with his black bow tie, and his head was adorned with what looked to be a tartan tam-o'-shanter. It set him apart from every other guest, all of whom were bedecked in more traditional evening wear. It was clear that he enjoyed holding court, for a small band of younger men appeared to be hanging on his every word. When he eventually saw Holmes and I, he broke free and approached us with an ebullient welcome.

"Gentlemen, you have arrived in good time. All my colleagues from the Paradol Chamber are here somewhere. Ah! There is Nicholas Lamboray, perhaps we should start with him."

What followed was an awkward twenty minutes of being dragged from one side of the hall to the other to meet the five. We both made polite small talk, and I realised how accomplished Holmes could be in feigning interest in people with whom he had not the slightest interest. It was only when I began to talk for a second time with Sir Peter Daines, that I realised Holmes was no longer by my side and had left the room.

I had known my dear friend to be stealthy on many of our adventures together, but that night he excelled himself. It could not have been more than seven or eight minutes since I had first noticed his absence, when I turned to find Holmes by my side once more. While pretending to wave across the room at one of the other guests, he whispered that he had managed to get to the second floor and had picked the lock to Cattermole's office, where he had seen the three forged paintings. Taking a sip of Champagne from a glass he had just accepted from a tall, blonde waitress, he then added: "Very well executed they are, too!"

We spent a few moments re-engaging with Kildare to avert any suspicions he might have had about our movements. I asked him his views on the Norwich School of painters that I particularly favoured, and he talked at length about the considerable talents of both John Crome and John

Sell Cotman. In doing so, he seemed not to notice Holmes's departure.

My final conversation was a second encounter with Damian Gastineau, a decidedly seedy and furtive old man with a foul mouth to match. The time was fast approaching seven-thirty and Holmes had yet to reappear. Four doors where opened off the main ballroom and many of the members began to file towards these. Gastineau cast a glance at one of the passing waitresses and winked lasciviously. He then turned to me. "Now the fun begins, doctor. It's such a shame that you'll not be here to sample the delights on offer."

He walked away towards a door which already seemed to be attracting a lot of interest. I glanced towards it and could see two or three scantily clad young women stood within the entrance having little trouble enticing the men in. I had no doubt that each of the other rooms had its own unique inducements. As my gaze fell upon the back of Anthony Kildare for the final time, I felt a hand touch my elbow and a familiar voice whisper in my ear. "It's done, Watson. Time to go."

****

It need hardly be stated that Holmes's conjecture on the scheme being perpetrated by Anthony Kildare proved to be accurate in every respect. On the flat roof of Wellington House, he discovered that a maintenance room used to house the essential workings of the building's heating system had been filled with all the paraphernalia required to produce his noxious gas. A gas line ran from the building to a small, double-barrelled air pump which sat close to the skylight. From this ran a shorter, more flexible piece of hosing – the means by which the phosphine gas could be hand-pumped down into the boardroom.

The meeting of the Paradol Chamber had been arranged for two-thirty on the Tuesday. We played our part in assembling in the boardroom alongside the others, reintroducing ourselves and again making small talk. In his chairing role, Kildare indicated that he had asked us to attend in order that we might observe the conduct of the meeting. The members did not seem unduly bothered. A moment later he announced that he would suspend the meeting for just a few short minutes as he had forgotten to bring with him his full set of minutes from the previous meeting. He invited everyone present to refresh their coffee cups and then left the room. I chanced a glance at Holmes, who merely smiled. We both knew that the boardroom doors were now locked, and Kildare would be making for the roof.

To ensure that no one was placed in any immediate danger, Inspector Lestrade worked with the ever-dependable Bill Hargreaves to have his officers secreted on each floor. So it was, that when Kildare reached the roof, entered the maintenance room, switched on the gas, and started up the air pump, he was greeted by two burly detectives from Scotland Yard who were only too pleased to place him in handcuffs and shut down his infernal device.

At the same time, the doors to the boardroom were unlocked by Lestrade who entered quickly, flanked by three more of his men. Their arrival caused some consternation and a few choice words from Nicholas Lamboray. Young Peregrine Cattermole looked close to tears, as both he and Lamboray were led away to face questions about their involvement in the art forgery scandal.

When we left the room, Holmes was able to assure the dutiful inspector that the three French oil paintings hanging along the corridor on the third floor were indeed forgeries. A subsequent search of Kildare's office revealed that his bags were already packed, including a map case housing the genuine canvasses. In a small travelling valise, the detectives also found a ticket for a channel crossing that very evening. Having killed everyone and made off with the stolen artwork, Kildare had planned to flee to the continent that very same day.

There was to be one final twist in the convoluted case of the Paradol Chamber. Having been tried at the Old Bailey, Kildare was sentenced to death for the murder of Mrs. Throckmorton and the attempted murder of eight others. Lamboray and Cattermole were each made to serve a minimum of seven years for their part in the art fraud. But on the day before his hanging, Kildare was found dead. He had used his influence to arrange for a kitchen knife to be smuggled into him and had slit his wrists, bleeding to death in his holding cell only hours before he was due to face the hangman. He left one final, pencil written note, which read simply: 'Death awaits us all – you too will go to Hell one day, Mr. Sherlock Holmes.'

Reflecting on the case after we had been notified of his death, Holmes poured us both a large brandy and sat before the fire. "Hubris can be a repellent trait, Watson. You may wish to remind me of that if I ever let my pride overrule my head in the way that Anthony Kildare did. Remember the words of Heraclitus, that 'character is destiny' - what you are largely dictates what you become. It is a simple adage that we would all do well to remember."

3. The Bewildered Blacksmith

During my long association with Mr. Sherlock Holmes there were to be a great many cases which I had not the time, energy, or inclination to commit to paper for the benefit of my readers. *The Bewildered Blacksmith* was an entirely different matter. While re-reading the correspondence which sets out the nature and narrative of that particular case, I realised that the addition of any words from my pen would be entirely frivolous. I believe the five letters which follow more than adequately tell the story without any unnecessary embellishment.

****

The Forge
Norwich Road
Chedgrave
Norfolk

Monday, 13th October 1890

Dear Mr. Holmes,

You will have to forgive the lack of formality with which I write this letter. I am not a literary man and sometimes struggle to set out my thoughts on paper. But the nature of the events that have bedevilled me in recent days has literally forced my hand. I therefore write to you in the hope that you can shed some light on what is a very bewildering and distressing matter.

Being based in Norfolk, it is no easy task for me to travel to London to see you in person. And as I begin to explain, you will understand why I do not feel able to leave my home at this time. So, let me get straight to the point and present you with the main facts and features of this peculiar affair.

I am a blacksmith by trade and inherited the business from my father, whose own father and grandfather before him worked the forge in which I operate. We are situated at the edge of a small village called Chedgrave. Being the only smithy for some miles around, I have a reliable and lucrative trade serving all the farms and small businesses across this area of south Norfolk. So much so, that I now employ a team of six men and manage the forge without having to get my own hands dirty, so to speak.

We produce everything from sickles and hoes, to ploughshares and gate hinges. But in the past six months, our biggest increase in trade has been in the production of hand-forged iron nails.

I now come to the incident which seems to have started this odd chain of events. I should explain that I am now in my mid-fifties and happily married to my wife, Frances, who is some six years younger. We have never been blessed with children, so I have for some time been considering who, within my existing workforce, I might eventually leave the business to. Anyway, that is by the by.

About three weeks ago I awoke one night convinced that I could hear footsteps on the gravel drive to our house. It was a cold, clear and moonlit night, and as I looked from our bedroom window, I saw a young man walking aimlessly towards the house, weary and bedraggled. He wore no hat or jacket and did not appear to have any boots or shoes on his feet. It took me some time to dress, and I also roused my wife, hastily trying to explain what I had seen. I then ventured from the house and walked briskly towards the forge.

I entered the main building with some trepidation, fearing that the young man might have ulterior motives for sneaking around at night. The forge within the shed is always kept alight, and the men have a system for banking up the coke at night to ensure that the fire never goes out. As such, the interior is always warm and bathed in a soft glow. As I looked around, I was a little shocked to see that the young man was curled up on some sacking on the floor beside the forge. And when I got closer, I realised that he was in fact fast asleep!

The poor lad was no more than seven or eight years of age and extremely thin. His unkempt dark hair was matted and greasy and his gaunt face streaked with dirt. The thick white shirt he wore looked to be three sizes too big for him, while his black trousers were, in contrast, too short for his long, skinny legs. Like his face, his bare feet and hands were filthy.

When my wife entered the forge and saw him, she could not help but weep, so pitiful was the figure laid out before us. She wasted no time in getting some thick blankets from the house to cover him and announced that she would sit with the boy until daylight to ensure that he came to no harm. I went back to bed, agreeing to take them some breakfast when I rose at six-thirty the next morning.

For the sake of brevity, I will not elaborate too much. In short, when the boy awoke the next day, he seemed bewildered and fearful. But due to the comforting presence of my wife and the offer of a cup of tea and a plate of cooked bacon and eggs, he soon began to relax. I have never seen a creature eat so heartily, Mr. Holmes, and it seemed clear to me that it had been some time since any food had passed his lips. The breakfast had a soporific effect, so much so, that having been carried from the forge and into the house he fell asleep once more on a rocking chair in front of the range and did not stir again until lunchtime.

We took steps to care for the boy. One of my men was despatched in a cart to bring a doctor over from Loddon. He examined the patient and declared that the lad was surprisingly healthy, yet clearly under-nourished and in need of a good bath. His teeth were good, and his limbs were straight, suggesting that it was only recently that the hunger had begun to take effect. Most surprisingly, the doctor announced that the boy was profoundly deaf, which helped to explain why the lad had, thus far, uttered no words when asked to give some account of himself.

Our local constable, PC Melrose, knew of no missing children and his enquiries confirmed that the boy was not a runaway from the local workhouse or the Norfolk Reformatory in Buxton, which is, in any case, over twenty miles away. With no further leads to pursue, Melrose suggested that the lad be taken to the workhouse – a plan which met with the immediate disapproval of my wife who declared that we would continue to look after him until such a time as his real parents could be found.

Both Frances and I have become very fond of our new lodger. Washed and dressed in fresh clothes, he is a handsome little fellow with a pleasant nature. And while we have not been able to draw from him anything of his previous life, he has been content to help with any chores we set him around the house. Beyond that, he has been reluctant to set foot outside the door and was positively terrified one day when we had a gentleman caller dressed in a frock coat and top hat.

PC Melrose has continued to make enquiries in the area, interviewing all the local shopkeepers, landlords and businesses, to see if anyone knows where the boy has come from. And while his appearance has sparked a lot of interest and a fair amount of speculation and gossip, no one has yet come forward with any reliable information. Without knowledge of his real identity, Frances and I had begun to call the boy 'Edward' – a name that we had agreed upon in the days when we still believed we might have a child of our own.

But now we come to the most distressing part of my narrative. Two nights ago, we turned in for the evening, having said goodnight to Edward. As we have but one upstairs bedroom, he had taken to sleeping on a makeshift bed within the kitchen, which is by far the warmest room in the house. I had checked that all the doors downstairs were locked. Yet when my wife arose the next morning and went into the kitchen to wake Edward, she found the bolts to the back door unlocked and our young lodger gone.

The local constabulary are as baffled as we are but are firmly of the view that the boy has simply returned home, having decided that he could not stay with us after all. I remain unconvinced and observed one other curious feature which made me believe that Edward was coerced into opening the back door before being abducted that night. Beyond the gravel at the top end of our drive is a small section of muddy track which adjoins the main road into Loddon. In searching for Edward before the police arrived, I saw the impression of thin carriage wheels imprinted in the soft mud, as if some vehicle had turned around in the drive before heading back to town. The width of the carriage tracks was very narrow and quite unlike those of the trade carts which usually come to the forge. Despite my protestations, it was not enough to persuade PC Melrose later that the matter warranted further investigation.

I know that you are not an agency for tracing children that have gone missing, Mr. Holmes, but I feel certain that there is something sinister about this whole affair. My wife and I will not rest easily until we know that Edward is safe. I therefore implore you to look into this matter for us and set our minds at rest. We will be pleased to pay whatever fees you deem necessary to secure such an outcome.

Yours sincerely,

David Goulding

****

The Forge
Norwich Road
Chedgrave
Norfolk

Wednesday, 15th October 1890

Dear Mr. Holmes,

Thank you for your telegram which arrived earlier today. I cannot begin to tell you how pleased and relieved my wife and I are to hear that you will be looking into this matter for us. And we are delighted to learn that you have already asked your colleague, Dr. Watson, to travel up to Norfolk first thing tomorrow to assist us. He will be more than comfortable lodging at *The Swan* in Loddon for it is indeed a fine hotel.

As well as thanking you, I felt it necessary to keep you apprised of developments since my first letter. While we have no further clue as to the whereabouts of young Edward, there have been other odd things happening within the village.

Yesterday, I took some time to walk to the rectory to enquire after the vicar of Chedgrave, the Rev. Bill Roper. While I am by no means a religious man and rarely attend church, I have some affection for Rev. Roper who was a good friend to my parents when they were alive. He has been poorly and confined to his bed for a good three months now, and there was some talk locally that the eighty-two-year-old might be on his last legs. While conversing with his wife – and learning that the amiable clergyman is rallying and making something of a recovery – I could not help but ask if Mrs. Roper had heard anything of the missing boy. She confirmed that she had not, but then uttered something very curious.

"You know that he's not the first strange child to appear in the village?"

I must have looked rather shocked and felt a little irritated that she had referred to Edward in such a manner. She went on to explain that five months earlier she had gone into Loddon to collect a wedding bouquet from Miss Hamer, the florist on High Street. While being attended to, she heard a noise towards the back of the shop and saw a young child emerge from a door behind the main counter. Knowing that Miss Hamer had never married and believing therefore that she had no children of her own, Mrs. Roper had asked who the pretty auburn-haired girl was. Miss Hamer then flushed and gave the vicar's wife some garbled story about the shy five-year-old being the daughter of her late-sister who had died of pneumonia the previous winter. With no other relatives to go to, Miss Hamer had apparently taken the girl in, with every intention of raising her as her own. Beyond this, the florist would speak no more and had looked visibly agitated.

I have to say that I could see no parallel between the unexpected appearance of Edward and the story of this foundling who now resided with the florist. Without wishing to appear rude to the elderly Mrs. Roper, I asked why she believed the story to be a fabrication. Her answer ran as follows: "I knew Miss Hamer had grown up in Bungay, for she mentioned it to me more than once. A couple of weeks after the encounter in the shop, my husband received a visit from the rector of St Mary's in Ditchingham. I happened to mention Miss Hamer to him, and he said at once that he remembered her family, who had been somewhat troublesome and had lived originally on the outskirts of Bungay, close to his parish. The father ran a local bakery and had been a heavy drinker. He became so unpopular within the parish that he was forced to sell up and move on, taking on the large shop and outbuildings that Miss Hamer now occupies in Loddon. The rector had not seen any of them since that time.

"Of course, I asked him how many children had been in the Hamer family, to which he replied, 'Two – an older son, Thomas, and Bethany herself, who was four years younger.'"

Mrs. Roper's conclusion was that the florist's story was a lie, but she had no theory as to why the spinster should concoct such a tale. Rather tentatively, I suggested that she may have had maternal instincts despite never having married and had perhaps taken in an orphan from the workhouse – something she had been embarrassed to admit. With some vitriol, the dour Mrs. Roper put paid to such a notion: "That woman has not a single nurturing instinct or caring bone in her body! I have never seen her do anything but chide any children who have dared to venture into her shop unattended. That will not do, Mr. Goulding!"

I let the matter rest and returned to what I thought would be a more comfortable line of enquiry. "Has the Reverend requested any help from the Bishop given his incapacity?"

Mrs. Roper seemed to find the question objectionable. "No, he has not. Young Mr. Allen, the curate, is quite capable of delivering all the regular services and sermons and attends to most pastoral matters. Why would you ask such a question?"

I felt uncomfortable but sought to explain: "The forge has been busy recently producing iron nails for Mr. Hoddy, the carpenter and undertaker in Loddon. I am grateful for his trade – for he is, by far, our biggest customer - and last week asked him casually why he needed so many nails. He indicated that there had been something of an increase in the number of old folk dying recently, and said that as he worked alone, he was finding it difficult to keep up with the demand for new coffins. Remembering that, it made me wonder if the church had struggled to deal with all of the funerals, as I know that the Reverend insists on doing all of the burial services himself."

Mrs. Roper had then looked somewhat bemused. "There have been no requests for burials since my husband became ill. In fact, I think I'm right in saying that the last funeral at the church was ten or eleven months ago. If there has been a steep increase in deaths, Mr. Goulding, they have not been in this parish!"

I said no more. And returning home, I relayed the story to my wife, who could see nothing remarkable about the account of the child at the florist's or Mr. Hoddy's pronouncement about deaths in the area. "He probably organises funerals for over a dozen of the local parishes. The burials could have occurred elsewhere," she said, bringing the conversation to a close.

While I found the revelations at the rectory to be a little unsettling, you can imagine my consternation when I was then told by my wife that a letter had been hand-delivered to our door. The missive came in a plain white envelope, addressed simply to "Mr. Goulding." Inside was a single sheet on which were stuck some words that had clearly been cut from a newspaper. The message read:

"Forget the boy he is safe if you persist it will be bad for you"

The cut-out letters were a mix of upper and lower case and there was no punctuation. In fact, rather than trying to describe the note further, I will enclose it with the envelope so that you can conduct your own analysis. Knowing of your skills, Mr. Holmes, it may reveal further clues as to the identity of the sender.

My wife and I have mixed feelings about the message. While there is some comfort in hearing that Edward is likely to be "safe", we are deeply troubled by the explicit threat and cannot shake the notion that the boy is in the charge of someone who does not have his best interests at heart. It hardly seems like the sort of note a parent would write.

While we can only speculate as to the identity of the author, there was at least one clue as to the person who had delivered the note. My intuition, having discussed the matter with my wife, was to head back down the drive. And I was glad I did, for in the soft mud at the entrance to our property were further impressions of the same thin carriage wheels I had seen four days earlier – the track of each being no more than two inches wide. I am now convinced that the owner of the carriage is the person who has taken Edward.

In closing, I must thank you once more for agreeing to help us. As you can imagine, we are eagerly awaiting the arrival of Dr. Watson.

Yours sincerely,

David Goulding

****

The Swan Hotel
Church Plain
Loddon
Norfolk

Thursday, 16th October 1890

Dear Holmes,

I trust you are well. I have already been remarkably busy since arriving in Norfolk but have made some particularly good progress as I will attempt to outline.

The journey to Loddon was not straightforward. My original plan was to travel on the first train to Norwich, to then find a road or rail route to the town. Having no station of its own, Loddon sits only a few miles from a halt at Reedham but disembarking at that point would have required me to make a ferry crossing to reach the market town! Having spent some time scrutinising my Bradshaw, I opted to travel on the Great Eastern line to Tivetshall, where I then caught a small train on the Waveney Valley line to reach a place called Geldeston. A hired dog cart served to carry me the remaining five or six miles and I finally reached *The Swan* hotel a little after eleven o'clock this morning.

I had but a few minutes to deposit my bags in the small suite of rooms that I took at the hotel, before heading out in the dog cart once more. A short while later I was set down at the top of the drive leading to the forge in Chedgrave.

Mr. and Mrs. Goulding could not have been more welcoming. He is a little over six feet in height with short greying hair, a lean figure, and something of a stoop. His good wife is a foot shorter, very much greyer, and sturdily built. Learning that I had set off from London at some unearthly hour, she insisted that I partake of an early luncheon. While Mr. Goulding gave me a quick tour of the forge, she prepared the meal – a plate stacked with an abundance of rural produce: cold pheasant, pickled onions, a slice of game pie, some thickly-cut brown bread and a sizeable wedge of cheddar cheese. A tall glass of homemade cider completed the meal.

While I ate, Mr. Goulding took me through the events of the previous day; the encounter with Mrs. Roper and the receipt of the threatening note. He explained that he had written to you with the same information. Fully appraised and unable to eat any more of Mrs. Goulding's fine food, I thanked them for their hospitality and announced that I would need to head back into Loddon to begin my discreet enquiries. They seemed reassured that I was taking such an approach.

It was only a short walk back into Loddon and I made the hotel my first port of call. It was as well that I did, for the reception desk had taken receipt of the telegram you had sent to me only an hour before. I was therefore able to follow up on some of the leads you suggested.

I went first to the business premises of James Hoddy on George Lane. He operates from a large yard, which is really a ramshackle collection of outbuildings and a small two-up, two-down cottage, which serves as the office for the funeral business. To the right of the entrance is a good-sized coach house and stable block, but it appears that most of the other buildings are used for woodworking, as I could see one open shed containing seasoned planks and timber and another housing some completed wooden packing crates.

Straight away, I was able to answer one of your queries. The street map of Loddon, which you say you were able to scrutinise back in Baker Street, was not misleading, for the George Lane yard sits directly behind the florists on the High Street. In fact, I could see immediately that the two had originally been one large plot as there were no boundary walls or fences between them. The path leading to the cottage continues beyond the building to the back entrance of a much larger structure, which I ascertained later to be Miss Hamer's.

I had only just entered Hoddy's yard when I was confronted by the man, who emerged from the shed containing the wooden crates. He was dressed in a long black frock coat, tall hat, and pressed grey trousers, which I imagined to be his undertaker's attire. He eyed me with some suspicion but greeted me pleasantly enough. In the background I could hear the faint sound of woodworking – at least one hand saw being used and a knocking from elsewhere. The sounds were strangely muffled and seemed to be coming from deep inside the building.

I explained that I had travelled up from London to visit my elderly mother, who resided in the nearby village of Hales. I said that while it was very distressing to me, I believed she had but weeks to live, and I had been forced to consider what funeral arrangements might be required. Hoddy's demeanour changed visibly in learning that I was a potential customer. I was shepherded into the office and the man began to outline the burial options and choices of coffin available to me. He seemed a little vexed to learn that I was extremely thrifty, and my mother had always insisted on having an inexpensive funeral. On hearing this, he pointed me in the direction of a roughly made casket, the cheapest coffin he sold. In looking at it, I had no doubt that the iron nails used in its construction had been produced at Goulding's forge.

Before leaving him, I asked if he could write down for me the principal details we had discussed and the costs of such a funeral plan. The tall Scot was only too pleased to do so. I've kept the small sheet of paper he used and will enclose it with this letter.

From Hoddy's yard, I walked back down George Lane and turned right onto the High Street. Bethany Hamer's shop is a substantial building with two large bay-fronted windows and an eye-catching array of plants and flowers. I learned later that it had once been a chemists with a full laboratory in the cellar. The florist herself was polite, but aloof, a little over five feet eight inches in height, with sandy-coloured hair and a world-weary demeanour. Her features could not be described as pretty, but there is something striking about her clear blue eyes.

For convenience, I stuck to the same story about my ailing mother and made general enquiries about the types of flowers required for a small family funeral and the likely cost of these. It was quite clear to me that Miss Hamer is something of a perfectionist. She uses only the best cut flowers for such occasions, the supply of which comes from a weekly delivery of blooms sent up from Covent Garden. When I expressed some surprise at this, I was told that she has a brother in London who attends the flower market and buys all the flowers she requests. These are packed into wooden crates for the rail journey to Geldeston, where they are then collected by cart.

During my time there I did not see or hear anything of the auburn-haired girl that Mrs. Roper claimed to have seen. But I did have one final breakthrough. In asking Miss Hamer to provide me with a list of suitable flowers and their respective prices, I was able to obtain a sheet of the paper she looks to be using for all the correspondence in the shop.

After this, I returned to the hotel and continued my enquiries. While enjoying a light evening meal and a splendid bottle of Beaujolais in the restaurant, I was able to glean some information from one of the older waitresses. Persisting with the ruse about my ailing mother, I mentioned that I had visited Mr. Hoddy and Miss Hamer that afternoon and was minded to use their services. I then asked if she knew anything of their reliability and reputation. She smiled warmly and replied: "You'll have no trouble with either, as both are very professional." She then moved a little closer and lowered her voice. "They do say that Mr. Hoddy has become quite sweet on Miss Hamer. He originally rented his yard from her, but six months ago they struck some sort of deal. He provides the wooden crates for her flower deliveries. He takes the empty crates to the railway station on a Thursday night, together with an envelope containing her order for that week. The full boxes are then returned the next day and Hoddy picks them up from Geldeston in his heavy cart. The arrangement suits them both. He pays no rent and she gets free deliveries."

"How do you know all of this?" I then enquired. The waitress beamed and gave me a sly wink. "Hoddy used to frequent *The King's Head* most evenings. I remember the night he told everyone about the deal. It was drinks all round, which was not like him at all. Then as the weeks passed, he stopped going out. Everyone believes that Miss Hamer has bewitched him."

"So, she is not a popular woman, then?" I could not help but ask.

"No," came the reply. "She is something of a recluse and has a wicked tongue. But to be fair, her flowers are the best for miles around."

There was more tittle-tattle about Miss Hamer and her shop. When I left the restaurant, I realised that it was still relatively early. And being a Thursday, Hoddy would be making the journey to Geldeston in his cart. I believed that if I could find out where the envelope and wooden crates were to be delivered, I could establish the London address of Miss Hamer's brother. Instinctively, I felt that might be relevant to the case.

I had in mind to visit the carpenter once again and explain that I had been told of his regular trip. As part of my ruse, I then planned to ask if it might be possible for me to accompany him, pretending that I had left one of my travelling cases at the station and was keen to retrieve it. I set off towards George Lane and as I approached Hoddy's premises could see a large tumbril cart sat in the entrance, headed by a powerful looking Shire horse. In the back were a dozen or more wooden packing crates, some with holes drilled in them. The yard was well lit, but I could see no sign of Hoddy. Confident that my subterfuge would work, I strolled up to the cart and began to gently pat the horse. As I did so, I could see that two of the crates had distinct address labels attached to them which read: *T. Hamer, 96 Worship Street, Shoreditch, London'*.

Realising that I no longer needed to continue with the charade, I began to edge backwards towards the entrance, listening attentively and watching for any sign of the carpenter. I cast a quick glance to my right and saw that the door to the coach house was partly open. Inside was an ornate black hearse and stabling for two further horses – clearly the stock of Hoddy's trade.

Back at the hotel, I decided to pen these lines to you rather than wait until the morning. I'm hoping that the hotel can organise for the post to be carried on tomorrow's milk train to London. That way, you should have my report by lunchtime and will be able to despatch a telegram with any further instructions you wish me to act upon.

In the meantime, I remain, your ever-loyal companion,

Watson

****

The Swan Hotel
Church Plain
Loddon
Norfolk

Friday, 17th October 1890

Dear Holmes,

It has been a remarkably successful day!

I spent some time with Mr. and Mrs. Goulding first thing this morning and gave them an outline of our progress. Both were shocked and saddened to learn that James Hoddy and Bethany Hamer are likely to be at the centre of this intrigue. They could not understand what motivations the pair might have for abducting children. At that stage, I did not feel able to share with them my thoughts on the matter.

Having walked back into Loddon, I then followed up on one of the other leads you had asked me to consider. There are three schools and one workhouse in the Loddon and Chedgrave area and I visited each. During the past year, none have taken in any auburn-haired girls of the age suggested by Mrs. Roper and there were no pupils or residents registered under the name 'Hamer.' Furthermore, none of the shopkeepers and business owners on the High Street knew of any child that lodged with Miss Hamer. The waitress at *The Swan*, who has proved to be a fount of local knowledge, also knew of no child, and scoffed at the idea of the florist becoming a stepmother.

After this, I turned my attention to the local clergy, starting with the vicar of the *Holy Trinity* in Loddon. Once again, I had to pretend that I was making enquiries about a possible funeral. I have to say that I felt distinctly uncomfortable lying to a man of the cloth but could think of no other way. During the conversation I asked about the number of funerals that had taken place at the church in the last year. The answer was "One." With the aid of a hired trap, I then visited a further eight parish churches and met with the same response – namely, that there has been no significant rise (or indeed, fall) in the numbers of people dying in the vicinity. I think it is fair to conclude that there has been no increased demand for Mr. Hoddy's coffins.

It was late in the afternoon when I returned to the hotel to find your telegram waiting for me. I was a little surprised to learn that you wished me to act so swiftly but did as you suggested and went straight to the police station in Loddon. There I located a ruddy-faced PC Melrose, who was overjoyed to learn that Mr. Sherlock Holmes required his assistance! Based on what you asked me to tell him, he agreed to accompany me to Hoddy's yard, together with another constable from the station.

At my request, PC Cleary was tasked with knocking at the door to Miss Hamer's shop on the High Street, while Melrose and I made our way to the George Street entrance of Hoddy's yard. The operation which followed could not have gone smoother, and as I write this can confirm that both James Hoddy and Bethany Hamer are now in custody at the police station and due to appear before the Loddon magistrates on Monday morning. They are to be examined on charges of child abduction, false imprisonment, and the passing of stolen goods.

I will await your explanation as to the full nature of the criminal enterprise being perpetrated by the pair, but already feel that I have a good understanding of what has been going on. At this stage, I will limit myself to describing exactly what we found at the premises.

The woodshed and storage buildings in the yard clearly demonstrated that Hoddy has been primarily engaged in the construction of large and small wooden boxes and crates, rather than coffins. In fact, across the whole of the site, we found only four completed coffins, whereas the number of crates numbered close to seventy. All but a handful had delivery labels attached to them with the same Shoreditch address I had seen on two crates the previous evening.

In Hoddy's coach house and stable block, I was able to examine the wheels of both the trade cart and the black hearse. The wheels of the cart were a good six inches wide, whereas those of the hearse were closer to two inches in width. I was able to take two small samples of mud from the wheels of the hearse, which I will bring back to Baker Street on my return to London.

When I mentioned to you in my earlier letter that I believed Miss Hamer to be something of a perfectionist, I could not have been more accurate. One section of the coach house had been set aside for the incoming crates which Hoddy had evidently picked up from the Geldeston railway station only a short time prior to our arrival. These had been carefully sorted into two distinct piles, with those containing Miss Hamer's flowers stacked to the left, while the heavier of the boxes sat unopened to our right. The latter all had delivery labels addressed to *'James Hoddy, Carpenter, George Street, Loddon.'* These were later found to contain many hundreds of leather-bound, books, manuscripts, and bibles.

Hoddy himself was arrested in his office, unaware that we had been quietly searching the outbuildings for some minutes before making our way to the cottage. He was in the process of preparing a pot of tea on a small log burner and was clearly shaken to see the bulky figure of PC Melrose pass through the door behind me. While he later refused to answer any questions about the activities he had been engaged in, he put up no resistance when told he was to be taken to the police station.

Bethany Hamer proved to be more of a challenge. When PC Cleary first knocked on the door to her shop, he was initially prevented from entering the building, with Miss Hamer claiming that he had no business there. It was only with his persistent knocking that the florist eventually agreed to unlock the door and let him in. And despite her acerbic protests he then began a thorough search of the house.

PC Melrose and I led the handcuffed James Hoddy to the back door of the florist's shop. Finding it unlocked, we entered the glass-roofed conservatory and were able to make our way through to the central section of the house. As we approached the main stairwell, PC Cleary was descending with an irate Miss Hamer following close behind. She froze when she saw the three of us and glared at the handcuffs on

Mr. Hoddy's wrists. PC Cleary then said that he had seen nothing out of the ordinary during his search of the upper and lower floors of the house.

It was then that I remembered something the waitress at *The Swan* had told me about the history of the shop. Specifically, that it had once been a chemists with a full laboratory in the cellar. With PC Cleary keeping a close eye on Miss Hamer and Melrose doing the same with her accomplice, I began the search for some sort of entrance to the underground room. And beneath a sizeable rug in the main parlour I soon found a trap door and stairway into what looked like a large and well-lit room below.

I descended the stairs with some trepidation, unsure as to what I might find. All the gaslights in the room appeared to be on. The first section of the cellar was full of woodworking benches and carpentry tools, all of which had been placed methodically on hooks and pegs along the walls. A couple of half-completed packing crates sat to one side, beyond which were two sawhorses and a neat stack of timber planks. It was only when I had walked beyond these that I realised there was a small door on the left at the end of the space. Opening the door slowly and with some cautiousness, I could already see that this room was also lit.

I was not prepared for the sight that then greeted me. Along the far wall of this much smaller chamber was some filthy-looking bedding on which were laid two young boys, each no older than eight or nine years in age. Both wore large white shirts and black trousers but had no shoes or socks on their feet. They looked towards me with evident surprise and the smaller of the two immediately began to sob quietly as if some misfortune were about to befall the pair. I smiled and did my best to quell any fears they might have, explaining that I was there to rescue them. The small boy continued to weep.

We did not find any further children, and there were no clues as to the whereabouts of the auburn-haired girl which Mrs. Roper claimed to have seen. Alongside the two adults, the boys were taken to the police station. After refusing to answer any of the questions put to them, Hamer and Hoddy were placed in separate cells and told that they would be re-questioned the following morning.

We treated the boys to a fish and chip supper and with the aid of PC Melrose's wife, Mary, were able to find them some clean clothes and boots which they changed into after bathing in my suite at *The Swan*. Returning them to the police station later, PC Melrose and I did our best to ask the boys about their imprisonment, but neither seemed able to communicate. It soon became clear to me that the smaller of the boys was deaf and was the 'Edward' that Mr. and Mrs. Goulding had taken in. The other boy appeared to be suffering from aphasia and his inability to speak could be the result of a head injury, brain infection or some form of psychological disorder.

PC Melrose was unsure what to do with the boys. He seemed relieved when I suggested that Mr. and Mrs. Goulding might take them in, given that they had already established some rapport with Edward. So it was resolved that we would requisition Hoddy's cart and PC Cleary would transport us out to the forge at Chedgrave. The constable had, in any case, to arrange for the George Lane site to be secured and some provision to be made for the horses.

As you can imagine, the Gouldings were overjoyed at the return of young Edward and had no qualms about taking in the second boy. They thanked me for all that I had done in finding him and expressed their heartfelt appreciation for your intervention in the case. Before I left, I explained that you would be writing to them to explain all the pertinent facts behind the affair. I hope that I have not exceeded my brief in doing so!

I should mention that I also managed to collect a small sample of the soil from the entrance to the forge, which I will bring back with me.

I will be returning to London tomorrow and should be with you sometime after midday. At that point, I hope you will be able to provide me with a full account of all that has occurred and how you ascertained that Hamer and Hoddy were the guilty parties.

In the meantime, I remain, your ever-loyal companion,

Watson

****

221B Baker Street
Marylebone
London

Saturday, 18th October 1890

Dear Mr. Goulding,

I'm delighted to say that the very unusual case which you brought to my attention only a few days ago has proved to be a stimulating and rewarding affair. I am grateful to you, for its resolution has been beneficial to us both, as I will now explain.

Dr. Watson returned to London this morning and has since briefed me on all the events which occurred yesterday. I am indebted to him for the sterling work he has done in resolving the case so decisively. You will be aware that James Hoddy and Bethany Hamer remain in custody facing several charges, including that of child abduction and false imprisonment. I have since had a telegram from the Chief Constable of Norfolk to say that both are likely to be remanded by the Loddon magistrates to appear at the next quarter session, where they will face the more serious charge of passing stolen goods. Such is the nature of our curious judicial system.

Firstly, and most importantly, young 'Edward' has been returned to you and your wife. I imagine that must be a great relief. The telegram from Norfolk Constabulary indicated that every effort will be made to trace the families of both boys. However, for the moment, they are content for them to remain in your care, if that is what you wish. If the boys are found to be orphans, steps could then be taken to make you their legal custodians.

Since their arrest, Hoddy and Hamer have refused to cooperate with the local police. However, I can tell you that Miss Hamer's brother, Thomas, has been cooperating fully with my detective colleagues at Scotland Yard. He has exposed all the outstanding details in the case which I had been unable to ascertain prior to his detention. However, let me take you through the case as it unfolded.

Having received your first letter, I recognised immediately that the appearance and rapid *disappearance* of the young lad you described warranted attention. In my experience, children who are orphaned, homeless, vulnerable, or otherwise uncared for, rarely have carriages sent for them. Yet that is what the tracks left in the mud of your drive indicated. It was clear to me that someone had gone to a great deal of trouble to recapture the boy yet had no great affection for him. It was equally apparent from his appearance and attire, that Edward had suffered some mistreatment prior to his arrival at the forge – a situation from which he had been desperate to escape. But as the doctor's examination had revealed him to be "surprisingly healthy," I could surmise only that he had been detained against his will for a short period before making his escape. And while loath to jump to any conclusion, could see that this already looked like a case of abduction.

Pursuing that as a working hypothesis, I was inclined to believe that our abductor was well-heeled. Not only did he or she have access to a carriage but could use such transport while others slept. You mentioned that Edward had been troubled by the appearance of "a gentleman caller dressed in a frock coat and top hat." Had he imagined this to be his well-healed kidnapper?

There was one other detail in your first letter which intrigued me. Specifically, the increase in Mr. Hoddy's demand for hand-forged iron nails. Some facts can often seem inconsequential in the scheme of things, but this one kept entering my thoughts. And as I reflected on the nature of the man's work as both a carpenter *and an undertaker*, and then thought about our elusive abductor, well dressed, and driving a carriage, I believed that I had already discerned some link – principally that an undertaker would have some ceremonial carriage or hearse for his business. Watson later confirmed this with his second visit to George Lane. On his first, he had already seen Hoddy in his business attire – a frock coat and top hat.

In recent weeks, my work has required me to remain close to Baker Street, but I felt confident in despatching Watson to assist you. As I am sure you have gathered, he is in every sense a safe pair of hands. Even as he travelled to be with you, the case was moving on and I received your second letter.

The appearance of the "pretty auburn-haired girl" seemed to be too much of a coincidence. Of course, had she continued to be a feature of the Hamer household and a resident of the florist's shop that might have been an end to the matter, but Watson's enquiries suggested that the young child had disappeared (he subsequently learned that no such child had been registered at the local workhouse or in any of the schools nearby). As Bethany Hamer had no children of her own, and clearly did not have a deceased sister, this looked to be a second case of child abduction. So, was there any link between Mr. Hoddy and Miss Hamer I began to wonder?

The first clue here was one of geography. You had included within your correspondence the addresses for both the shop and the funeral parlour. Consulting my extensive collection of street maps, I determined that the George Lane location of Hoddy's business sat directly behind the florists on the High Street. Watson's enquiries later revealed that both had once been part of a single plot purchased by Miss Hamer's alcoholic father. Furthermore, we now know that Hoddy and Hamer had become emotionally attached.

That aside, there was a clear symbiosis in the way that the business relationship developed between them, beyond the fact that both were involved in the funeral trade. Thomas Hamer was already based in London and travelling to Covent Garden each week to purchase all the flowers his sister required. As her business grew, she needed more and more wooden crates to transport the flowers by train from London. Hoddy's arrival in Loddon provided her with just that, but he was also able to use his cart to pick up the flower boxes from the railway station at Geldeston, removing the need for her to employ a local haulier. Offering the carpenter the inducement of free rent must have seemed like an easy way to initiate him into the other, more sinister, activities that the Hamer siblings were engaged in, as I will explain shortly.

The second clue as to Bethany Hamer's role in this affair, came, somewhat unexpectedly, with the hand delivery of the threatening note, which you helpfully enclosed with your second letter. My examination revealed that while the notepaper was quite unremarkable, being cheaply manufactured and readily available in most stationers, there was one distinct area of staining on the paper which looked to have come from the thumbprint of the sender. Microscopic analysis of this revealed that the ochre staining had been caused by flower pollen – specifically the pollen of a lily.

Hearing that you had found a second set of carriage tracks at the entrance to the forge, I realised that Hoddy and Hamer must have been acting in concert. And when Watson later provided me with a handwritten quote from the florist – which had clearly been taken from the same pad as that used for the threatening note – I had a final confirmation of my supposition.

Furthermore, I now have proof that Hoddy's hearse travelled to the forge that second time. Watson was diligent in collecting soil samples from the carriage and your drive. My laboratory tests have confirmed these to be identical in their composition.

When Dr. Watson visited Hoddy's yard on Thursday evening he was able to provide me with a final and crucial piece of information. Namely, the Shoreditch address of Thomas Hamer, the real villain of this case. When I received Watson's letter yesterday, I acted with some haste. Assisted by Inspector Lestrade and other officers from Scotland Yard, we raided the warehouse premises of Mr. Hamer. As a result of what we discovered, I wasted no time in sending a final telegram to Watson. He was to use my name to secure the assistance of the Loddon police in arresting Bethany Hamer and James Hoddy. I wanted to be sure that when the wooden crates were transported from London and arrived in the carpenter's yard, we would then have all the proof we needed to show how this disreputable criminal enterprise worked.

By that stage, I was convinced that young Edward was being held in the cellar of the florist's shop together with at least one other person, possibly a second child. My suspicions had been aroused by Watson's first visit to Hoddy's yard. He could hear the muffled sound of woodworking – a hand saw being used and a knocking – and believed the noises to be coming from deep inside one of the buildings. From your earlier letter, I knew that Hoddy claimed to work alone, for he had said that he was finding it difficult to keep up with the demand for new coffins. So, who were these additional woodworkers? With Watson's description of the shop on the High Street, and the reference to the former chemist's laboratory in the cellar, I surmised that it would be the most likely and secure location to keep someone captive – a young child (or children) who were also being coerced into working for the carpenter.

Hoddy's assertion that there had been an increase in the demand for coffins, because of the rise in the number of deaths locally, appeared to be untrue. Watson's investigations proved as much. Hoddy needed all the additional iron nails to produce more and more wooden crates for the business that the Hamer siblings were engaged in. Not just the transportation of flowers from Covent Garden, but the active transportation of abducted children and stolen goods.

In short, Bethany and Thomas Hamer were running a 'baby farm.' Through her connections to the funeral trade,

Miss Hamer would often come across families who had lost their beloved children. Preying on their grief, she would offer to find them a similar child to erase the pain of their loss. If they were amenable to this, terms would be agreed, and Thomas Hamer would then be instructed to find and abduct a child matching the description provided by his sister. He would choose children who were homeless, destitute, or orphaned so as not to provoke too much suspicion when they disappeared. He used laudanum taken from the former laboratory in the cellar to drug the children and transported them by cart to his Shoreditch warehouse, where they would be packed into wooden cases for the journey to Norfolk. Heavily sedated, yet able to breathe through carefully drilled holes in the wooden cases, they would arrive at Geldeston and be picked up by Hoddy, together with the packed flowers and the crates of stolen goods. The regular nature of the consignments helped them to pass largely unnoticed on the rail route from London.

While thorough in procuring children as instructed, Thomas Hamer was not so meticulous in checking the nature of the youngsters he trafficked. When Edward arrived in Loddon, Bethany Hamer discovered that he was profoundly deaf and therefore unsuitable for the family he had been promised to. Similarly, when a second lad arrived a month later, he was found to have difficulties in speaking. In both cases, Hoddy took charge of the boys, putting them to work in his carpentry business and providing them with only meagre rations of food. At first, they were housed in the stables, but when Edward had been recaptured after his time with you at the forge, the boys were moved to the cellar of the florist's shop, which the criminals believed to be a more secure penitentiary.

Edward's escape proved to be unsettling for Miss Hamer, who felt that they were getting careless, particularly after the incident with Mrs. Roper and the sighting of the young auburn-haired girl. She made the decision to send the threatening note, convinced that you would be scared to pursue the matter, especially if you knew that Edward was, in any case, "safe." She clearly underestimated the lengths you were prepared to go to on Edward's behalf.

Children like the auburn-haired girl were sent on to their new families within one or two days of arriving in Loddon. Thomas Hamer confirmed that they had abducted nine children altogether, and – of the seven who were placed with families in Norfolk – the enterprise had generated an income of £420, which was split three ways between the Hamer siblings and James Hoddy.

While this was a very lucrative trade, it was not the mainstay of their criminal enterprise. That relied on a more traditional method of generating money. Thomas Hamer is something of an expert in rare manuscripts and books. Old bibles are his particular specialty. For the past five years he has orchestrated dozens of thefts across the country of rare book collections – in private homes, bookshops, and museums.

Each robbery was meticulously planned, with only the most desirable items taken. So much so, that Scotland Yard believed that the books and bibles were being stolen to order and shipped to customers only too willing to pay extraordinary sums to obtain the rarest of manuscripts. A month ago, two rare Venetian bibles were taken from the British Museum and the police could find no clues as to their whereabouts. I knew of the robbery but was engaged in two or three other cases which prevented me from assisting Scotland Yard – until, that is, your case took us to the Shoreditch address of Thomas Hamer.

When we descended on his premises, we discovered that he was none other than the notorious 'Tome Raider' of the London underworld. Inspector Lestrade still believes that I was hot on the heels of this infamous book thief in requesting his assistance. In reality, I believed we were pursuing a commonplace child abductor who had not been overly clever in covering his tracks. You will understand now why I said that the resolution of this case has been beneficial to us both!

Acting on the information provided by Thomas Hamer, the Norfolk Constabulary has now arrested four book collectors, all of whom were in possession of hundreds of stolen manuscripts and bibles. Scotland Yard is confident that with the cooperation of other forces around the Country, the bulk of the material stolen by Hamer over the past five years will be found and returned to its original owners.

So ends a fascinating and fruitful case. Given the very considerable credit I have received from Scotland Yard for assisting them in bringing the 'Tome Raider' to justice, it would be churlish of me to request any fees from you for my role in this affair. In any case, it was Dr. Watson who proved to be the real star in this investigation.

I have no doubt that we shall correspond further as the criminal proceedings play out in the coming weeks and months.

Yours sincerely,

Sherlock Holmes

****

Note: There was something of a postscript to this story. For some years after the case, David and Frances Goulding kept in touch with Holmes. They eventually became legal guardians to Edward and the second boy, whom they named 'William'. Both young men became accomplished blacksmiths, but also developed their skills in other areas. Edward learned to speak, although he remained profoundly deaf. He succeeded in becoming a successful author of children's books. William overcame the trauma he had suffered as a result of a blow to the head to become a fluent communicator, learning several other languages, including French and German. In later years, he worked as a tour guide in Berlin. When the Gouldings eventually died, the business was left to the adopted sons and Edward continued to run it as the 'Goulding Forge'. It became a major manufactory during the Great War producing metalwork for Britain's rapidly developing airship industry – JHW.

4. The Recalcitrant Rhymester

In writing up the exploits of my dear friend Sherlock Holmes, I fear I may have given the reader the misleading impression that all our adventures together were fascinating, colourful affairs, truly worthy of the consulting detective. In reality, many of the cases on which we were engaged proved to be far less interesting than he might have hoped for and barely worth recording for posterity. The narrative which follows might well have been one of those, had it not served as the last chapter in a long-running saga which had occupied Holmes for the better part of a year. For that reason alone, I believe it merits some attention.

Holmes and I had been asked to investigate a private matter at the end of September 1896. Thomas Jermyn, a West End theatre manager, had noticed for two weeks running that his takings had been significantly down on what he might have expected, given that his auditorium appeared to be filled most nights. Reluctant to turn to Scotland Yard - for fear that his somewhat seedy entertainment programme might be exposed to the full scrutiny of the law - he had asked Holmes to undertake a discreet enquiry. Somewhat to my surprise, the great detective took up the case with apparent relish.

The chief suspects were a disparate group: a one-legged doorman who had worked at the theatre for over ten years; an ageing showgirl who had previously worked the streets around Paddington Station; a ticket clerk who had only recently been employed; and a stage manager who had developed something of a gambling obsession. With little real effort, Holmes had easily determined that the latter had been pocketing a proportion of the theatre's takings each night to finance his poker habit. That man was Frederick Paget.

When Holmes put the matter to him that morning in the office of Thomas Jermyn, Paget did not deny that he was the thief, but began to plead with his employer to let him keep his job. He said he was desperate and owed a substantial sum of money to a major poker player who ran a popular card school in a country hotel some thirty miles north-west of London. If he could not pay off his debts, he feared for his life.

On hearing this, Holmes became strangely animated and silenced the theatre manager who had begun to say that Paget had no one to blame but himself and stood no chance of retaining his position. He addressed the thief very directly: "Is this country hotel the *King's Arms* coaching inn?"

Paget was visibly unnerved by the directness but responded clearly enough. "Yes, it's in the village of Amersham, in Buckinghamshire."

"And this poker player you owe money to...?"

"His name is Halvergate - Edwin Halvergate."

I realised immediately why Holmes had taken such an interest in what looked initially like a very trivial affair. For the past year, Halvergate had been a thorn in my colleague's side, teasing him with poetic conundrums alluding to real crimes but staying well out of reach of the law. Then, when Holmes had undermined his criminal operations by pitching him into an unwelcome turf war with the Italian families of the London underworld, Halvergate had been more explicit in his communiqués. Writing to the detective in early September, he said simply: "I will write up your obituary in sonnet form." Since that time there had been one clumsy attempt on Holmes's life and a botched break-in at 221B.

Holmes said nothing of this to the two men, but did take Thomas Jermyn to one side, urging him to continue to retain the services of his stage manager for at least a week. Beyond that, he said the matter of the gambling debt would be resolved and the theatre manager could then decide for himself whether he still wished to dismiss Paget. With some reluctance, Jermyn consented, telling the stage manager that he was on his final warning and was not to do any more gambling.

In a cab travelling back to Baker Street, Holmes explained his reasons for looking into the theft at the theatre. "I have known for some time that Paget has been a regular at the gaming table of Halvergate. The Baker Street Irregulars have done a thorough job of watching all the comings and goings at the coaching inn in recent months. What I could not be sure of, was whether the fellow was a trusted criminal associate or just another hoodwinked poker player. Our investigations at the theatre have proved him to be the latter and the invitation to look into the matter could not have come at a better time."

"But I don't understand why Halvergate has suddenly placed himself at the centre of a gaming operation so far from town. It all seems a bit parochial. You told me earlier this year that he was the head of a powerful criminal gang operating out of Seven Dials, with aspirations to expand their activities to other cities across England."

"All true. But our little intervention in the Faccini murder case has created considerable problems for this one-time sidekick to Professor Moriarty. In placating the Italian families, he has had to relocate from London and pay over substantial sums of money. In short, they have bled him dry, and he is now attempting to replenish the gang's empty coffers before reasserting his authority within the Capital's criminal fraternity. That I am the architect of his downfall has not gone unnoticed. My plan is to strike again while the man is temporarily weakened and to end his illicit activities once and for all."

I was not sure whether this was brave or foolhardy on Holmes's part but had to trust his judgement. As we pulled up to the pavement outside 221B, I asked, "What's the plan from here?"

"I have some immediate matters to attend to, but suggest we then dress for the evening and take the Metropolitan Railway out to Amersham. I favour a few hands of poker in a country inn. What say you, Watson?"

****

The *King's Arms* proved to be a sizeable hostelry in the centre of the old village of Amersham, just over a mile from the railway station. We arrived a little after seven-thirty to see an expensive private carriage draw up at the well-lit entrance. It was clear from the crest and monogram on the door of the four-wheeler that the establishment was attracting a few well-heeled patrons.

Holmes stepped forward as the coachman's assistant opened the door. A tall, elegant man in a top hat stepped down from the carriage. He had a long angular face and deep-set hazel eyes framed beneath a dark brow. A large black overcoat with a thick astrakhan collar covered most of his body down to the ankles. And on his feet he wore a pair of thin-soled elastic-sided boots. Seeing my colleague, his face lit up. "Mr. Holmes! What a pleasure indeed. Are you to join us at the card table?"

"That is my intention, Lord Cranhurst. I am something of an infrequent gambler but cannot resist a hand or two every now and then." He turned and beckoned toward me. "I'm not sure whether you have met my close friend Dr. Watson?"

Cranhurst moved toward me and extended a gloved hand. "I have not, but am delighted to make your acquaintance, Doctor. I have read so many of your excellent tales. Holmes and I go back some way – in fact, he once helped me to resolve a particularly sensitive criminal matter. So you might say we share an interest in sleuthing."

I exchanged some pleasantries so as not to appear discourteous but wondered at the wisdom of talking so openly given our mission. If Holmes had hoped to arrive incognito and to remain inconspicuous, his plans looked to be scuppered. Stood on either side of the entrance were two broad-shouldered doormen, each dressed in a smartly tailored white tunic and neatly pressed black trousers. A look passed between them, before the smaller of the two turned and headed off into the hostelry. The second greeted us with a polite, "Good evening, Gentlemen," while holding the door open to allow the three of us to enter. From there we were ushered towards a small side room where we were able to deposit our coats, hats, gloves, and sticks.

What followed during the next few minutes can only be described as farcical. It was quite clear from Halvergate's reaction that the would-be criminal mastermind was completely flummoxed by our appearance.

During our rail journey, Holmes had indicated that apart from a handful of bar staff, employed purely to serve drinks, Halvergate had retained only six close associates as part of his criminal enterprise. We were shepherded into a large dining room at the rear of the inn, at the centre of which sat a sizeable oval table bedecked with all the paraphernalia required for the poker game. Halvergate was already positioned at one end of the table, away to our left. He smiled uneasily as we entered and nodded for the broad-shouldered doorman - who had no doubt alerted him to our arrival - to return to his colleague outside. A quick reconnaissance showed that there were a further four, well-dressed, and extremely muscular, men positioned around the room – the remainder of Halvergate's foot soldiers.

The man himself was somewhat shorter than I had expected, perhaps five feet, six inches in height, slender in build and gaunt in the face. His grey eyes were darkly ringed, and his head topped with a heavily oiled crown of thin and silvering hair. I put his age at close to fifty years and observed that he had a slight tremor in his right hand, which seemed only to intensify the more he chose to glance across at Holmes.

Halvergate greeted Lord Cranhurst in an effusive tone and began to introduce him to the three other men who were already seated at the table. In summary, these were a merchant banker from Surrey, a stockbroker newly arrived from Chicago, and a self-made colliery owner who ordinarily resided in Nottinghamshire. Holmes and I received a less demonstrative welcome but were nevertheless addressed cordially and offered a seat at the gaming table. I declined the offer, preferring, instead, to be seated in a far corner of the room close to a serving hatch connected to the main bar. This meant that the poker school was now comprised of six men.

We were offered complimentary drinks and I readily accepted a small glass of single malt whisky, more to steady my nerves than any genuine desire for refreshment. Holmes, I noted, asked only for an ashtray, so that he might smoke one of the small cheroots he pulled from a silver case in his side pocket. One of the well-tailored associates slid the desired item on to the table beside him. As he did so, his right forearm was exposed sufficiently to reveal a small tattoo – the wasp symbol under which Halvergate's men operated. The man then returned to a standing position against the wall opposite me.

With the introductions completed, Halvergate addressed the players around the table, outlining the house rules for the poker game. One or two queries were answered quickly, before another of the associates took his place at the end of the table opposite Halvergate and assumed the role of dealer. Each player then declared how much he would like to draw down in poker chips before the game commenced.

It is not my intention to provide you with a blow-by-blow account of the scrimmage which followed, but, after a period of some three hours, it was quite clear who the winners and losers were. For all their supposed professional expertise, the banker and stockbroker had sustained the heaviest losses – by my crude reckoning somewhere close to forty pounds apiece. The colliery owner was out of pocket by around half of that amount. Lord Cranhurst had played cautiously and opportunistically to minimise his losses, which I guessed to be about five pounds. For his part, Holmes looked to be up by some seven pounds, the neat piles of poker chips in front of him having grown steadily as hand after hand was played out.

By far the clearest winner was Halvergate, whose composure had not changed throughout the game. There was no hint of conceit as he announced quietly that it had been an honourable and well-played game, which had, inevitably, left some "a little out of pocket".

I was surprised that the remark did not elicit any negative responses from the men now rising from the table, seemingly content to hide their disappointments and to disappear quietly into the night. In fact, it was Holmes, who, while remaining seated, turned to Halvergate, and announced curtly: "I cannot agree that this has been an 'honourable' game, Sir. 'Well-played' on your part, certainly, but not within the realms of any acceptable gaming conduct. I put it to you, that you are a cheat, and have deceived these good men as you have the many others who have passed through this illicit gaming establishment in recent months."

Even by Holmes's standards, this was a bold and provocative move. Halvergate's four associates looked primed and ready for action before their leader raised a hand, smiled enigmatically, and asked that all but my colleague and I be accompanied outside to the carriages awaiting their departure. This was achieved with no objections from the banker, stockbroker, and colliery owner. Only Lord Cranhurst opted to remain with us, stating that he wished to hear why Holmes believed the game to have been rigged.

It was a reflection of Halvergate's hubris that he now seemed prepared to act despite the obvious presence of Cranhurst. With two of his associates seeing to the departure of the other players, he directed the remaining men to search Holmes for any hidden weapons. Having roughed him up with no obvious result, they turned to me. My stubborn refusal to stand up and be patted down brought a sudden and painful punch to the head. Temporarily dazed, I was then held by the lapels of my jacket, with my head slumped forward, until my assailants were sure that I had nothing secreted about me. I was then flung back down into my chair.

Against his protestations, the two men then lurched toward Lord Cranhurst and removed him bodily from the room. For some moments afterwards there was the sound of a considerable scuffle outside. I imagined that the peer had continued to resist their attempts to eject him from the premises. On his own, Halvergate then sought to gain the upper hand, deftly removing a small pistol from the inside of his tweed jacket and pointing it at Holmes's head.

"You've been a thorn in my side for some considerable time now, Mr. Holmes. How ironic that it should come to this. You couldn't have made it easier for me to be rid of you, along with your lap dog here..." He cast me a glance, his eyes now burning with hatred and his gun hand shaking almost uncontrollably. "I'll finally get to finish what my former mentor was unable to achieve!"

Holmes rounded on him without any apparent fear. "You're no match for Professor Moriarty. Not even a close second fiddle. Despite the animosity between us, I relished the mental stimulation I had in battling with the man. In comparison, you are nothing but a petty criminal and an obsessive narcissist." He shouted suddenly: "Go ahead, use that single shot in your pistol. Then take your chances with Dr. Watson!"

I realised then that the raised voice was but a signal. The door was flung open and in raced a posse of uniformed police constables led by a red-faced inspector. Close behind them was a concerned-looking Lord Cranhurst. Halvergate was genuinely dumbfounded by the commotion. It was only when one of the constables grabbed his right forearm and began to wrestle the pistol from his grip that he seemed able to rationalise what had just occurred.

"I might have known that you'd bring your Scotland Yard chums with you, Holmes! Couldn't fight me on your own, eh?"

Holmes flashed him a mischievous grin. "I'd save the sarcasm, Halvergate. Inspector Hopkins here is indeed from the Metropolitan Force, but the other officers are from the Buckinghamshire Constabulary. Including Sergeant McClean, who was masquerading as Lord Cranhurst. I imagine that he has already arranged for your criminal associates to be hand-cuffed and taken into custody."

"I'm not interested in your charades," exclaimed Halvergate. "And I think you'll have trouble securing any sort of conviction for anything I've done here tonight. I'll argue that I drew that gun in self-defence. If you didn't already know, I have a particularly good solicitor that I keep on a particularly expensive retainer."

It was at this point that two more police constables entered the room, one carrying a stack of files and ledger books, the other in possession of some heavy looking cash boxes. Inspector Hopkins pointed for the items to be placed on the oval table.

Holmes seemed to be relishing the drama. "Oh, don't think for one moment that these officers are interested in your low-level poker scams. They have no intention of putting you before a jury to explain how you have been counting cards and using mirrors, a marked deck and coded signals from your henchmen, to dupe the hundreds of card players who have sat at this table. No, their interest is in something more fundamental. I think they will even be prepared to overlook the display with the pistol. Perhaps you could explain, Inspector Hopkins?"

Stanley Hopkins stepped forward keenly and looked Halvergate up and down. "Finally, we meet on my terms. Scotland Yard has spent months trying to find a way to reel you in. But I knew that if I planned any sort of official raid it would be destined to fail as you have some very highly placed informants within our ranks. And that costly solicitor of yours would intervene to scupper our investigations. But Mr. Holmes devised a very neat strategy. He suggested that we contact our colleagues in the Buckinghamshire Force who have responsibility for this part of the country. Sergeant McClean was most obliging and arranged for a dozen of his finest officers to accompany me here tonight. He even offered to go under cover, to ensure that no harm came to Mr. Holmes and Dr. Watson. They, of course, were placing themselves in the lion's den, given your recent threats. But Mr. Holmes reasoned that this bold approach would keep you and the bulk of your associates in this room while we went exploring..."

Halvergate snorted unexpectedly. "How very astute – and I'm touched that you've gone to so much trouble. But I fear that it will lead you nowhere. Search this building all you like. You'll find no stolen goods, no secret cache of weapons, nothing, in fact, which will point to any underworld activity. You've had a wasted journey."

"Not in the least," replied Hopkins. "Mr. Holmes made it quite clear that we would be unlikely to find anything that would point to your usual shady dealings. You were tutored by Professor Moriarty, after all. No, what we were looking for resides in the ledger books and cash boxes that now sit on that table. In your desperate quest to raise money to maintain some sort of toehold in the metropolis, Mr. Holmes reasoned that you were likely to be engaged in all sorts of fraud, tax evasion and false accounting. And a quick look at those files and books earlier suggests that he was absolutely right."

It was Holmes who now spoke: "I suspect you have overlooked just how seriously Her Majesty's Treasury is likely to view your financial indiscretions. I'm certain that a long prison sentence will be the most likely outcome – as well as the seizure of all your assets. You know what our marvellous London prisons are like, Mr. Halvergate, particularly when you have no money to protect yourself. Still, a cultured man like you can probably make a few friends. Perhaps you can read them a few of your published poems..."

Halvergate launched himself at Holmes, escaping the clutches of the constables either side of him. He took a long and energetic swing at the head of my colleague, who reacted instinctively by parrying the blow with his right fist and following up with his left. The punch was enough to floor the card sharp, whose legs crumpled beneath him.

It took the best part of an hour for the police officers to finally clear the inn and ensure that they had not overlooked any evidence which might further incriminate Halvergate. The man himself was unceremoniously thrown to the floor of the police van which arrived to take the gang into custody.

With all the constables gone, the four of us sat in the main tap room. Inspector Hopkins helped himself to a bottle of brandy and some glasses from the bar and passed them around to McClean, Holmes, and me. He was fulsome in his praise for what we had all done in securing the gang's arrest.

"Is that likely to be the end of the matter?" I asked.

"Almost certainly," replied Holmes. "Halvergate will not come back from this and his men are all marked - those wasp tattoos will betray their allegiance. No rival gang will want to touch them given the ripples that Halvergate has created in the London underworld. The bigger question is who might now step forward to fill the void they will leave?"

Inspector Hopkins took a further nip from his brandy glass and smiled broadly. "All true, but that is a challenge for another day, Mr. Holmes. Let us just savour the moment. But I will say that you gave me something of a fright this evening. How did you know that Halvergate wouldn't pull that trigger at the first opportunity?"

A playful grin passed across my colleague's face. "In truth, I didn't. But as I said earlier to our bogus Lord Cranhurst, I am something of an infrequent gambler."

Sergeant McClean laughed heartily and offered his hand to me. I shook it and looked at him quizzically.

"Let us not forget Dr. Watson's part in all of this. He played a blinder himself. There aren't many men who would take a beating for a comrade. He might easily have been shot."

"Indeed," concurred Holmes. "Let's drink to Watson."

****

It was many months before Edwin Halvergate was finally to appear before a judge and jury charged with multiples counts of fraud and false accounting. Despite the expensive retainer, his legal adviser could do little but try to minimise the sentence which his client was likely to receive.

In the event, his legal shenanigans proved unnecessary. On the evening before the judge was due to pronounce sentence, the recalcitrant rhymester was found dead in his prison cell. With a ripped sheet taken from the bed, he had hanged himself from one of the bars covering the small window of the cell.

There was one further postscript to the story. On the Wednesday following Halvergate's death, Holmes received an unexpected letter. It contained a single sheet of foolscap bearing the letterhead of Newgate Prison. On it was written in pencil a short haiku verse. It read simply:

"Edwin hoped to win.
Holmes – he was the better man.
No more games to play."

5. The Groaning Stone

"This looks like a lively affair, Watson!" said Holmes, thrusting a folded copy of *The Times* into my lap. "A dead body, a missing ring and a mysterious note. And the detective leading the investigation is said to be 'baffled'. We will no doubt be hearing from Inspector Bradstreet within the hour."

I had to that point been reading the first chapter of Henry James's novel, *The Portrait of a Lady*. But with Holmes's evident exuberance, I placed the slim volume aside and began to scan the newspaper under the heading 'Renowned Botanist Dead – Police Suspect Foul Play'. Yet I had read no more than the opening paragraph of the piece when I was distracted by a loud knocking on the door of 221B.

"Bradstreet is quick off the mark, Watson - his bafflement must be quite profound!"

We both laughed and prepared for the arrival of the dutiful inspector. Seconds later a light footfall could be heard on the stairs, and as I chanced to look across at Holmes realised that his expression had changed to one of confusion. He raised his eyebrows and shrugged his shoulders as we received a gentle rap on the study door.

"Please, do come in," said Holmes.

The lean, long-faced man who entered the consulting room was clearly not Inspector Bradstreet. In his early sixties, he had short greying hair and a thin moustache. And he must have read something of our expressions, for he looked quickly between us before saying, "I am seeking Mr. Sherlock

Holmes, but seem to have interrupted you in some way. Would you prefer me to call another time?"

His concern seemed to be wholly sincere and Holmes sought to reassure him. "Not at all, Mr. Faulkner. I am Sherlock Holmes, and this is my colleague, Dr. John Watson. We are at some point expecting a visit from a Scotland Yard detective and wrongly believed that it was he who was calling on us. As soon as you began to ascend the stairs, I realised my error, for you are a little lighter on your feet than B Division's Inspector Bradstreet."

This appeared to provide him with little by way of comfort. He smiled weakly and added: "I apologise for not arranging an appointment in advance, but I had to set off exceedingly early this morning. And you have the better of me already, sir – how did you know my name?"

Holmes beckoned for our client to be seated. "The initials 'C. Faulkner' are etched into the silver at the top of your walking cane, which I imagine was a gift from a former employer upon your retirement some eight years ago – the date is also visible you see. That you caught the milk train from your home in East Anglia is evident from the stub of the Great Eastern Railway ticket that is protruding slightly from the outside pocket of your frockcoat. Yet despite the early start, you took the time to walk your new puppy before catching the train. The black and white hairs still clinging to the lower leg of your trousers attest to this and the light teeth marks towards the bottom of the stick indicate that the canine in question is still in training. If I must be bold, I will surmise that your new puppy is a sheepdog."

His face lit up like that of a child seeing a magic trick for the first time. "Quite remarkable, Mr. Holmes! My name is Chester Faulkner, and I am a former accountant and widower, originally from Oxford. I settled in the small village of Lynford in Norfolk on my retirement in the late summer of 1888. Being alone, I have developed a new-found enthusiasm for walking and, with the acquisition of a sheepdog puppy named Gillespie, have taken to hiking around all of the local byways close to my home."

I interjected at this point. "Then it must be a matter of some concern which brings you to us today given the vulnerability of the young pup."

Faulkner nodded most assuredly. "Indeed, Doctor. Each year I make the journey to London to visit my bank manager who takes care of all my financial affairs. Today was that day. And yet when we had finished running through all the regular matters we needed to discuss, he said that I looked tired and somewhat preoccupied. I have known dear Mr. Dunn for many years, so decided to take him into my confidence and shared with him the matter which has troubled me in recent days. In seeking to resolve this, Dunn told me that I should visit 221B Baker Street and consult with a Mr. Sherlock Holmes and his colleague, Dr. Watson."

"I see," replied Holmes, seemingly bemused. "Then you must tell us more."

Faulkner nodded. "I would describe myself as a quiet, level-headed person, with a rational disposition, not given to flights of fancy. I was told that the pair of you have a reputation for solving puzzling conundrums. That being the case, I would very much welcome your help in providing me with a rational explanation for how a solid block of granite can be heard to groan at night."

It was not the opening gambit I had anticipated, and I fancied that I saw the corners of Holmes's mouth twitch in amusement at the introduction. He reached for his briar pipe and matches and relaxed back in his familiar chair before then giving our visitor his full attention. "Then you must furnish us with all the relevant facts, Mr. Faulkner, for this sounds like an intriguing affair. Please start at the beginning and be sure to leave out none of the salient points."

The man responded immediately and sat forward in the seat to deliver his narrative. "I live in a small cottage on West Tofts Lane, a mile or so outside Lynford. Two days ago, Gillespie and I had been confined indoors for the better part of the day as the weather had been both wet and stormy. But by the late afternoon the skies had cleared, and we were able to amble around in the forested land to the east of nearby Lynford Hall, a manor house and estate with centuries of history. It is an area I had not ventured into before and I found it quite enchanting, being full of tall, sweet-smelling spruce trees and abundant with wildlife. But with the failing light, we headed home, and I promised Gillespie that we would return later that evening with a lantern to guide our endeavours.

"With our supper finished, I spent some time tidying up and then gave Gillespie the customary signal that our adventures were to resume – I had only to pick up the red lead to his collar for him to spring into action and race eagerly towards the front door.

"It was a mild evening which barely warranted the thick overcoat and scarf that I had chosen to put on. We set off briskly and had only been walking for about two minutes when I saw my nearest neighbour, Harold Boyes, strolling some distance ahead of us. His cottage lies a little further along West Tofts Lane. Boyes is in his mid-eighties, but is surprisingly sprightly, and has a passion for wild orchids. I shouted out to him, but he seemed not to hear me and was soon out of our sight. The only other person we saw before reaching the forest was Jenny Cowgill, who runs the local bakery and is also something of an herbalist. As she approached us on the path, I could see she was carrying a basket brim full of plant leaves, herbs, and fungi. I wished her a 'good evening' but received only a nod of the head in reply – a response not untypical of the spinster, who rarely attends any of the events and activities which occur in the village.

"We retraced our way through to the forest and began to walk on further than we had previously. While it was helpful to have a lantern for the darker sections of the forest's interior, the landscape at the edge of the trees was bathed in vibrant blue moonlight and revealed a track running in a wide arc to our left. We ventured onto this and continued for a mile or so until we came to a break in the trees and a short descent into a more open area of woodland, populated with traditional oak trees. We found ourselves in a wide pit, almost like a natural amphitheatre, through the centre of which ran our path.

"The canopy of the wood was less dense than that of the forest and we had no trouble seeing the way ahead. Presently, we came to an open patch of short grassland, perhaps twenty feet across, in which sat a single and most peculiar stone. It was roughly dome-shaped, perhaps five feet wide at its base, and rising upwards to a height close to my own chest. Examining it at close quarters, I saw that it was a naturally-occurring granite boulder which I imagined to be an 'erratic' stone, moved to its present position by the shifting plates of frozen water which covered the landscape during the period we now refer to as the Ice Age."

Holmes raised a hand and interposed. "Up to this time, had you seen or heard anyone else on your travels beyond the earlier encounters with Mr. Boyes and Mrs. Cowgill?"

"No. We were quite alone, and it was eerily quiet. I stood back to admire the stone, lit up as it was in the moonlight.

And as I did so, Gillespie began to growl quietly, his own eyes fixed on the boulder. It was then that we heard it – a low groaning noise, unlike any sound I had ever encountered, which continued for eight or nine seconds before stopping as abruptly as it had started. I could only think that the noise had been made by something behind the stone. However, it did not take long to dispel that idea, for Gillespie clearly had the same notion – he began to circle the stone, continuing his low growl and pacing frantically. He looked visibly agitated when he could not detect the source of the groaning.

"The next sound we heard was equally unnerving and completely unexpected. To this point, I had not realised that we were still within reasonable distance of the estate. Loudly chiming out the time of ten o'clock, we heard some familiar bells which I knew to be those of the private Catholic chapel which sits in the grounds of Lynford Hall. The stone remained silent, and both Gillespie and I waited for some minutes before turning and wending our way home."

"What were your immediate thoughts, Mr. Faulkner - had you no further clue as to the nature of the noise you heard?" asked Holmes.

The retired accountant reflected on the question and then answered him directly. "I was completely unnerved by the experience and could see no logical explanation. My immediate concern was to get home safely, and I put Gillespie on his lead so that he would remain close to me. Our progress was slow as I was desperate to ensure that we did not lose our way. Within twenty yards of the cottage, we had just a mud track to cross. Distracted by the dark thoughts swirling around in my head, I was about to step forward when Gillespie gave a short, sharp 'yap,' pulled me back from the track, and then sat upright by my side. I stopped instinctively and glanced down at him. His head was inclined to the right, and as I followed his gaze, I was stunned to see a heavy cart pulled by two dark horses almost upon us, travelling at speed. Without slowing, it passed within two feet of us and continued on its way before then turning right into the village."

"Was the noise of the cart anything like the groaning sound you heard earlier?" I enquired.

"Not at all, but its appearance seemed strange at that time of night and only added to my general uneasiness."

"I see," replied Holmes. "Yet by your own admission, you are a *level-headed person, with a rational disposition, not given to flights of fancy.* So, I imagine you visited the stone a second time?"

"You have the measure of me, Mr. Holmes. Despite my initial reservations, I set out again last night with Gillespie at my side. I was confident that we would find an obvious explanation for the groaning stone. The only person we saw on the way was the herbalist, Jenny Cowgill. She was someway off in the distance and looked to be picking some fungi from the base of a large elm tree."

Holmes regarded him keenly. "Did you have any reason to believe that her reappearance had any bearing on the matter?"

"No. I mention it only for completeness as you asked me to earlier."

"Indeed. And what happened after that?"

"Well, it was close to half-past nine as we approached the stone, the only sounds to that point being the screeching of a barn owl and the distant barking of a fox. Yet we had barely time to stand within six feet of the boulder before the groaning began afresh, the deep moaning sound seeming to reverberate in the very ground beneath our feet. I was petrified and stood rooted to the spot, the sound continuing for a good ten seconds before stopping, to be heard no more. Gillespie was similarly affected and seemed relieved when I finally moved back from the clearing and turned for home.

"When we reached the safety of the cottage, I sat for a couple of minutes in a chair close to the fire, struggling to make sense of what we had again experienced. Gillespie jumped up onto the window seat which faces the front gate and began suddenly to whimper. I stood to see what was troubling him. As I did so, there was a loud rumbling outside, and as we both peered out of the window, I saw the same vehicle and horses that had passed us so closely the previous night. I could just make out the dark shapes of two men sitting up in the cart."

"Did you have any suspicions as to the identity of the pair?" I asked, still struggling to grasp the nature of the case being presented to us and its relevant features.

"No, Doctor. But I cannot help but think their appearance has some bearing on the matter."

Holmes stepped forward from his chair and began to lightly tap out the contents of his pipe into the hearth of the fire. "Have there been any further developments since that time?"

Faulkner looked somewhat sheepish as he responded. "No. And I hope you do not think me delusional when I say that I am now convinced that the stone holds some dark power, and I would be wise to avoid any further contact with it. But I cannot sit by without knowing what lies behind its strange attempts at communication. I therefore implore you to come to my aid, Mr. Holmes. I will happily pay you whatever fee you deem necessary to cover your time and expenses."

It was a heartfelt plea and somewhat to my surprise Holmes readily agreed to investigate the matter, albeit with one important caveat. "We will happily take the case, but I suspect that Scotland Yard is likely to require my assistance in the capital over the coming days. If he is agreeable, I would like to suggest that Dr. Watson travels up to Norfolk tomorrow to begin the investigation."

I was a little bemused, but otherwise comfortable with the proposal. It meant shifting a couple of appointments, but realising it had been some weeks since I had enjoyed anything approaching a break from work, felt that a short excursion might be a welcome relief. Chester Faulkner was delighted when I agreed to the proposal.

Our client left us a few minutes later. With his departure, Holmes gave me his early thoughts on the matter: "While this seems like a highly convoluted affair, I am certain that at its heart lies a very straightforward explanation for this mysterious moaning stone. The key will be in sorting the wheat from the chaff. Follow all the leads you can, Watson, and we will see what comes of it. I'll do my best to assist if you can keep me informed of your progress by letter or telegram."

I was about to respond when I heard a further knock at the door downstairs. Holmes jumped to his feet with unmistakable enthusiasm. "Now, that must be Bradstreet! Let us hear what he has to share with us."

So began *The Mystery of the Groaning Stone* and *The Case of the Butchered Botanist*. As it transpired, I was to have little to do with the latter – a case which Holmes managed to lay to rest within a day of Bradstreet's visit. For my part, I left

221B just after lunch and made plans to travel up to Norfolk the following day.

****

I set off early that Wednesday to travel by rail to Ely. From there, I was able to catch a smaller Great Eastern train to Brandon in Suffolk. Being some four miles north-east of the station, I had to hire a dog cart to transport me on the final leg of my journey across the county border to Lynford in Norfolk. The driver said my best chance of finding local accommodation was to try *The Crown Hotel* in nearby Mundford. By the time I reached the hotel and had successfully secured a room it was a little beyond midday. I found the hotel to be pleasant enough and its food and ale most agreeable.

After lunch, I began to scout out the geography of the area. Mundford was less than two miles from Lynford Hall – a splendid neo-Jacobean manor house set within acres of forested estate land. It had been rebuilt a few decades earlier by Stephens Lyne-Stephens, then the richest commoner in England, who died before the work could be completed. He had been married to the French ballerina Yolande Marie-Louise de Verney, who had died only two years previously. She had paid for the private chapel on the estate – a fine piece of religious architecture, built at huge cost with locally-sourced flint. It was the bells from this that Chester Faulkner had heard during his first encounter with the groaning stone. I discovered that they chime loudly on the hour.

I was able to find out the history of the estate by chatting to one of the groundsmen at the hall. He said that the property was currently unoccupied, with the solicitors continuing to sort out the probate on Mrs. de Verney's estate – as a widow, she had died without children and had no immediate heirs. Given this situation, the number of staff working at the hall had been significantly reduced, to the extent that there was just a housekeeper and maid working within the house during the day, while two groundsmen tended to the gardens and estate. He said that the hall had originally employed closer to twenty staff all told.

The groundsman was able to point me in the direction of the mysterious stone. I set off along a track from the rear of the chapel towards some dense woodland. At that back of this I found a steep incline to the open area of ground which Mr. Faulkner had described. There were large stones scattered throughout the woodland, the floor of which was uneven and hard to negotiate. The area looked to have been a quarry at one time and a separate track from the site appeared to be heading off in the direction of Lynford village.

When I reached the stone in question, I was surprised to see that it was a different type of rock to those in the woodland below. The granite had clearly been worked to give it its distinct dome-like shape. And from its position I concluded that the stone had been placed there deliberately - the view down over the estate being quite stunning.

Despite spending a good fifteen minutes scrutinising the area around the stone, I could find nothing to explain the groaning noises that our client claimed to have heard. And it did not oblige me by emitting any sounds of its own. I decided then that I would try to find the route to Faulkner's cottage based on the description he had given. This proved to be straightforward enough and a short while later I reached the track running past his property.

The man himself was most welcoming and his dog, Gillespie, proved to be a real bundle of joy. Over a cup of tea, Faulkner explained that a lot had happened since his return from London the previous day. I invited him to tell me all the pertinent facts.

Perched on the edge of his Chesterfield sofa, he began: "After travelling from Brandon by cart, I arrived back in the village about four o'clock. With a few chores to complete, I began to ask as many people as I could about the stone. Very few of the locals appeared to know of its existence, although a few fellow dog walkers acknowledged that they had seen it but had not experienced anything unusual in doing so. Most believed the boulder to be no more than a way marker or a folly placed there by one of Lynford Hall's previous owners.

"Only one person offered up an explanation for the mysterious groaning. This was Mr. Catchpole, the builders' merchant, who looked visibly shocked when he overheard my conversation with Mr. Stevens, the local postmaster. He said the boulder had been worshipped by the ancient druids and being a pagan stone, groaned at night to the chimes of the chapel clock on the Lynford estate. He added that anyone hearing it should not visit the stone for a second time as it would almost certainly bring them bad luck – it had been cursed for centuries. As you might imagine, it was not the sort of explanation I wanted to hear."

"Indeed," I replied, somewhat incredulous at the thought.

"Yet, Mr. Stevens, the postmaster, laughed at the revelation and said he did not believe a word of it, advising me to do the same. He made it clear that his family had lived in the area for generations and he had never heard anything about the stone being worshipped or cursed. Mr. Catchpole became quite agitated by the rebuke and said that if we did not believe him, we should consult with Mr. Parsons, the local carter, who would tell us the self-same story. He was resolute in the face of Stevens's continued mockery and stormed off before I could speak to him further."

I asked Faulkner what had occurred after that and he resumed his narrative: "I confess that I was more than a little vexed by Catchpole's revelation. For it is fair to say that since then I have had further troubles. Yesterday evening, I heard the heavy cart for a third time. After my trip to London, I decided to have an early night and was in bed by nine o'clock. Gillespie roused me from my slumber about an hour later by barking at something outside. I put on my dressing gown and came downstairs to find Gillespie sat upright on the window seat, still barking. And as I approached the window, I heard the low rumble of the cart and watched once more as it passed by with its two passengers. Unfortunately, I could see nothing of their features.

"This morning I awoke to find that the gate to the cottage had been wrenched from its hinges. Bushes had been trampled and my stone sundial had fallen over – even though it is too heavy to have been toppled by the wind. And I discovered a maggot-infested crow on the doorstep. All of which I see as bad omens. It was as if some powerful force had swept in off the track, attempting to lay waste to my garden."

I continued to be somewhat sceptical of the whole narrative but could see Faulkner was genuinely upset in relaying the story. After making a fresh pot of tea and offering me a slice of Victoria sponge, he continued: "I wanted to confirm Mr. Catchpole's story about the groaning stone, so set off this morning with Gillespie at my side. My first port of call was the bakery in the village. While I had not thought to speak to her earlier, it struck me that as an herbalist Mrs. Cowgill was more than likely to know of any local folklore regarding the stone. Yet my straightforward question along those lines prompted only a curt 'No'.

"I then called on Mr. Parsons, the carter. He has a large ramshackle yard on the outskirts of the village where he keeps all his horse-drawn vehicles. These are used mainly to transport farm crops and livestock from the village to the station at Brandon. I found the man near the stables, a big burly fellow with a thick neck, balding head, and ruddy complexion. Despite what I knew of his reputation as a brusque, unyielding character, I found him to be pleasant enough and he did not seem at all surprised or perturbed by my enquiry. 'Aye, that's right,' he bellowed, 'that stone is cursed, and they do say that anyone visiting it more than once, who is not of the druidical faith, will incur the wrath of the pagan gods and suffer some misfortune. It is not to be tampered with. My advice to you, Mr. Faulkner, is to stay indoors at night rather than traipsing about in the woods.'

"He said this without any apparent malice, and his words were accompanied by a gentle smile. I thanked him and returned home. Yet I could not shake the notion that there were still dark forces at work. And as I reflected on what Parsons had said, it struck me that his advice had been rather curious. For in asking him about the stone, I had said nothing of my night-time visits to it. In fact, the only people who knew that Gillespie and I had seen the boulder in the dark were Mr. Catchpole and Mr. Stevens. As the former had been the first person to mention the alleged curse, I speculated that he and the haulier must be in league. Furthermore, I now wonder whether the heavy cart that has passed the cottage for the past three nights belongs to Mr. Parsons."

I listened to this with growing interest. And for the first time began to feel that there might be a genuine case underpinning this mystery. *Was it possible that Catchpole and Parsons were up to no good and the story about the druidical stone was just a ruse to keep Faulkner from revisiting the area near the stone?*

I left the cottage a short while later, promising to return the following day. But before leaving West Tofts Lane, I paid a visit to the home of Harold Boyes, whom Faulkner had recalled seeing during his first encounter with the stone. I explained that I was a friend of Faulkner's, staying locally, with a keen interest in the local landscape. I asked him if he knew anything of the druidical stone near Lynford Hall. He was friendly and open in his response, saying only that while he had passed the stone many times in his quest for wild orchids, he knew nothing of its origins, or any stories connected with it. From my brief discussion I concluded that I could safely rule out Boyes as any sort of suspect. Sprightly though he was, he had not the build to wrench gates off their hinges or to push over heavy stone sundials. It was also clear that he was profoundly deaf and had to lip read all that I said. If there had been a groaning stone, Harold Boyes would certainly not have heard it.

Back at the hotel, I had a brief conversation with the manager, Mr. Shaw. This revealed that while he did not know Mr. Catchpole, he was fully acquainted with Mr. Parsons. The hotel had occasionally used him to transport guests' heavy packing cases to and from the railway station but had stopped doing so when one particular case went missing and Parsons refused to reimburse the guest concerned. The manager had heard others in the village say that the man could be both 'light-fingered' and unreliable.

In the early evening, I set down a summary of all that I had discovered in a letter to Holmes. Mr. Shaw said that he could arrange for the envelope to be taken to Brandon later that evening – the mail being transported on the last train to London. That way Holmes would receive it in the first post and could respond with any further instructions or enquiries by telegram.

****

I awoke the following morning to see that the day promised to be both sunny and warm. And after a delicious cooked breakfast, set off into the village to continue my enquiries.

I went first to the bakery run by Mrs. Cowgill. She was a little frosty to begin with but warmed when I explained that I was a doctor researching the scope for using more traditional hedgerow remedies in my medical practice and had been told that she was a talented herbalist. We chatted for a good twenty minutes about her favourite concoctions and she seemed happy to share her extensive knowledge. At one point, she mentioned the healing properties of fairy ring champignon. I expressed some surprise and said that I thought I had seen some growing around a granite boulder on a site overlooking Lynford Hall. She agreed that this was entirely possible but said that she was unable to confirm the sighting as it had been a good two years since she had ventured that far into the forest – most of her ingredients were gathered in the woods close to West Tofts Lane.

I then walked to Mr. Parsons's yard on the outskirts of Lynford and realised that I had passed by the premises on my return to the hotel the previous evening. As such, it was on the direct route out of the village towards both Lynford Hall and West Tofts Lane.

On the pretence that I was seeking to transport some timber to Thetford, I spoke to Parsons and had a quick look around his premises. His manner was abrupt, and I got the distinct impression that either he did not believe a word of my story, or he did not want my trade. The yard contained many vehicles and stabling for over a dozen horses. But it was something of a shambles and most of his wagons looked to be filthy – the cart he suggested for the timber was not only mud-spattered but appeared to be covered in a thick layer of white dust. When I asked if he would be able to transport the wood that evening, he said he could not oblige me as he already had a paying customer.

With the time fast-approaching ten o'clock, I returned briefly to the hotel to see if Holmes had sent any word. I was rewarded with a broad smile and a positive affirmation from the pretty receptionist in the foyer: "Yes, Dr. Watson, a telegram was received about ten minutes ago."

I was delighted to learn that Holmes was no longer required in London and was setting off to travel up to Brandon. His train was due at 11.34 and he asked me to book him a room at the hotel and to hire some transport to meet him at the station. With the assistance of the receptionist, this was all done within minutes and only a short time later I was bouncing along in a dog cart enjoying the splendid, forested scenery on the road to the station.

For a small rural halt, Brandon station was surprisingly busy. The London train pulled in a minute early and it was some moments before I spotted Holmes with his overnight bag. He had evidently seen me already, for he gave a cheery wave of his hand in which he was clutching his well-worn travelling cap. I gave him a broad grin in return, and when I reached him offered instinctively to take the bag from his hand.

"Thank you, Watson, but I think I can manage." We walked along the platform and out of the station to where the dog cart was waiting. I had just enough time to brief Holmes on my visits that morning and he listened intently to all that I had to say.

With his bag placed safely beneath his seat, Holmes was about to ask the driver to set off, when he raised his hand and announced suddenly that wished to speak to the station master. The driver raised no objection, particularly as my colleague had already offered to pay extra for the time incurred. I waited in the cart. It was a good five minutes before he returned looking decidedly pleased with himself.

As the cart rattled its way back towards Mundford he explained his actions. "It occurred to me that the station seems to be the dropping off point for all of the traffic in these parts. You told me about Parsons, the local carter. If we are to assume that he is in league with Catchpole and making frequent night-time journeys for nefarious purposes, I wondered whether the spoils from their work might be finding their way to Brandon for the onward journey to the capital or elsewhere. And it was a line of thought which bore some fruit!"

"How so?" I inquired, eager to know what he had learnt.

"The station master told me that Mr. Catchpole has been a frequent visitor there of late. For the past two months, he has been arranging for regular shipments of stone to be transported to London each Friday – sometimes in significant quantities. The station master was not sure what type of stone is being carried as it is always within sealed wooden cases. But it did strike him as odd. For the many years he has been acquainted with Catchpole, he has only ever known the builders' merchant to receive supplies *from* London, which he then sells to his customers. While he has tried to coax further information from Catchpole, the man has always remained tight-lipped about the shipments."

"Well it hardly seems like evidence of criminal activity - a builders' merchant transporting stone!"

"Then why all the secrecy and the late-night cart journeys? There's more to this, mark my words."

He turned his attention to another matter and began to tell me all about his work with Inspector Bradstreet on the case of the butchered botanist – a gruesome affair, in which Holmes had been able to identify the killer from a handprint left when the guilty man tripped up the stairs to an attic room. Holmes had already ascertained that the stair dimensions were not consistent, and the distinct difference between the rise on one step and the adjacent one following it had caused the killer to stumble, before steadying himself on a shiny wooden bannister. The unique scarring on the man's palm could be seen clearly in the resulting handprint, which proved to be the only physical clue to his presence at the time of the murder. Holmes finished his narrative as we approached *The Crown Hotel*. I made a mental note to write up the case as soon as we returned to London.

When my colleague had checked into the hotel, he announced that he had several tasks he wished to complete, including the despatch of some telegrams. He suggested I pay a second visit to the home of Chester Faulkner to inform him of our progress, and we arranged to meet back at the hotel around four o'clock.

The day had continued to be bright and it was a pleasant walk out to West Tofts Lane. As I approached Faulkner's cottage, I could already see that he was sat out in the front garden enjoying the warmth of the sun. Gillespie was sprawled out asleep by his side but woke immediately as I opened the newly fixed gate.

"Good afternoon, Dr. Watson!" said Faulkner. "May I get you some refreshment? I was about to make a pot of tea and treat myself to another slice of sponge. Could I tempt you with the same?"

"That would be splendid," I replied.

Once more, Faulkner proved to be very agreeable company. He was delighted to learn that Holmes had made the journey from London and was intrigued to hear that Catchpole had been transporting stone to the station at Brandon. He told me more about his time in Oxford and his late wife, who had been a talented opera singer. We talked for over two hours, at the end of which I returned to the hotel to see what Holmes had discovered.

I found him in the lounge bar of the hotel enjoying a pint of local ale and a thick ham sandwich. I ordered the same for myself and sat down. "In the short time since I left you, I have been remarkably busy," said he. "As well as sending and receiving a number of telegrams to an academic in Durham, I have visited the mysterious groaning stone and seen the location of the mine that I believe Catchpole and Parsons have been using to obtain the stone they have been sending by rail to London."

"Then you must have passed West Tofts Lane while I was with Faulkner."

"Indeed. And very cosy it looked too. I scouted around in the woods to the right of the cottage and kept out of view. I was keen to see the landscape for myself and draw this matter to a conclusion, before enlightening Mr. Faulkner."

"And have you achieved that?" I asked.

Holmes grinned. "We have but one final fact to corroborate."

"Which is?"

"We need to confirm, once and for all, that it *is* Catchpole and Parsons who are making the regular journeys out along the dirt track past Faulkner's cottage."

****

Later that afternoon we walked to Parson's yard to prove his theory. We were careful to remain out of sight and approached the premises through some dense woodland.

Close to the gates of the yard was a small thicket of bushes in which we were able to conceal ourselves. It was just as well, for we had only been there for seven or eight minutes when a man entered the yard and disappeared into one of the outbuildings near the stables. This I guessed to be Catchpole from a description Faulkner had given me. Presently, he reappeared in the company of Parsons, who began to hitch two powerful looking horses to the dust-covered cart I had seen earlier. Catchpole, meanwhile, began to wheel a large piece of machinery up a ramp into the back of the cart, which he then covered with a tarpaulin. Other pieces of equipment were also loaded before the cart pulled out of the yard some minutes later, heading off in the direction we had anticipated with both Parsons and Catchpole on board.

"We have our proof, Watson, and a bit more besides! Let us pay a final visit to Mr. Faulkner and put this matter to rest."

I was a little taken aback, for I was not sure that I had grasped all the salient facts. But knowing Holmes's methods, I trusted that he would explain all when we reached the cottage.

Chester Faulkner was thrilled when he opened the door and saw Holmes and me. And it was all we could do to get into the living room of the cottage without tripping over Gillespie, who ran between us wagging his tail excitedly.

When we were seated finally, Holmes began to explicate all that he had determined. "Mr. Faulkner, this has proved to be a stimulating and enlightening affair. In the event, its resolution was straightforward, but there were some fascinating points of interest as I will attempt to explain.

"The mystery began with your discovery of the granite boulder, or 'groaning stone' as you termed it. You believed it to be an 'erratic' boulder, moved to its present position by the movement of glaciers during the Ice Age. I am by no means an expert on the geology of the East Anglian landscape but seemed to remember that the counties of Norfolk and Suffolk have few, if any, naturally occurring rocks of that type. To be sure, I contacted an academic colleague. His name is Canon William Greenwell, an archaeologist who undertook an extensive survey of the landscape around Brandon between 1868 and 1870. Greenwell has assisted me on several cases where I have needed to understand the nature of rock formations. He was only too pleased to respond to my numerous telegrams, and, as it proved, his expertise was both unique and invaluable.

"Greenwell confirmed that the stone was almost certainly moved to its present position 'by the hand of man, rather than the hand of god' - as well as being a leading archaeologist, he is also a Church of England priest. Interestingly, he said that there is a direction marker or 'groaning stone' in Debenham, Suffolk, which is said to move and groan at midnight with the striking of the church clock. There are also plenty of so-called 'druid stones' in the east, marking spots of earlier pagan rituals and worship. However, Greenwell has little time for superstition and is firmly of the view that our stone was most likely moved there by James Nelthorpe, who purchased Lynford Hall from Sir Charles Turner in 1717, to create a 'folly' or feature of interest on his newly acquired estate.

"Greenwell was the first to discover the Neolithic – or *New Stone Age* – site of *Grime's Graves*, which sits only a few miles from Lynford Hall. The 91-acre site contains more than 400 shafts which were dug by these early settlers to reach the rich seams of flint which are embedded underground. The site was worked for more than 300 years from about 2,600 BC, the stone being used to make polished stone axes. And since that time, flint has been mined in the area for the purposes of building.

"I recalled that the Catholic chapel which sits within the grounds of the estate was also built of locally sourced flint. I therefore asked Greenwell whether it was possible that the quarry which Dr. Watson observed yesterday was evidence of another early flint mine. He said that this was almost certainly the case and speculated that the quarry might even be from the earlier Palaeolithic – or *Old Stone Age* – period.

"I realised at an early stage that the strange noises you heard around the stone must have come from below the earth. In fact, you said yourself that the sound seemed *to reverberate in the very ground beneath our feet*. So, the information about flint mining suggested to me that the underlying nature of the landscape might offer an explanation for the groaning sound.

"From the off, we had a number of suspects in the case. However, Dr Watson's visits to Mr. Boyes and Mrs. Cowgill, suggested that they were unlikely to be involved. In contrast, Messrs. Catchpole and Parsons have been acting suspiciously, and we were able to confirm that they have been visiting the quarry site each evening.

"When Catchpole heard that you had been walking around at night in the area close to the stone, he was fearful that you might discover what they have up to, which, for them, has been a very lucrative trade. In a clumsy attempt to scare you, and to keep you indoors at night, he invented the story about the groaning stone and the druidical curse. To reinforce this, the two men damaged your garden and placed the dead crow on your doorstep. There was no curse - Catchpole and Parsons are simply thieves, stealing from a quarry on the Lynford estate.

"With the death of Mrs. de Verney, Lynford Hall currently has no residents and only a few daytime staff. At night, it is deserted. The pair have been taking advantage of this, knowing that they can visit the quarry with little chance of being seen or stopped. Each evening they set off from Parsons's yard with all their mining equipment. And at ten o'clock, they finish their work when they hear the chimes of the private chapel on the estate, and then make the return journey.

"Every Friday, the product of their labour is transported in heavy crates to Brandon station. The stone is then taken to London where the recipient is only too willing to pay the going rate for the material. At first, I believed the two men were illicitly mining for flint but reflecting on Watson's observations about the cart being covered in a thick layer of white dust, realised my mistake. The track running from the quarry is littered with small bits of white stone and light-coloured dust – further confirmation that it is chalk, rather than flint, they have been mining. At present, chalk is highly sought after in the capital given the large numbers of new buildings being constructed in the city.

"Greenwell's information should have pointed me in the right direction much earlier, for the flint deposits in Norfolk are almost always found in chalk-rich areas. In fact, the archaeologist explained in one of his telegrams that more than 2,000 tons of chalk had to be excavated by Neolithic miners before they could reach sufficient quantities of flint. This represented the work of some 20 men, using picks made from red deer antlers, over a period of about five months.

"For Catchpole and Parsons, the extraction of the chalk has been a much easier process. They merely connect a pneumatic rock drill to the piston of a small, portable steam engine. Such drills have been in use across Europe and North America since the 1850s. With it they can mine significant quantities of the porous rock, which is worth a small fortune. And, of course, it was the operation of this heavy, steam-driven drill which created the 'groaning' noise you heard from the mine, which is located directly below the granite boulder, many feet underground."

He stopped at that point and I could see Faulkner was ecstatic. "Mr. Holmes, I cannot thank you and Dr. Watson enough. Your reputation is truly deserved. Now that you have explained it, the matter seems almost trivial in its simplicity. But how will you proceed? Will you seek to take action against the pair?"

Holmes shook his head. "Ultimately, that will be a matter for the police. I had planned to spend the night in Mundford, but still have time to catch a train from Brandon this evening. Knowing that Catchpole and Parsons will be transporting another shipment tomorrow morning, I have time to return to London and arrange for the Metropolitan Police to intercept the cargo. They will be able to contact Norfolk Constabulary who will then be able to arrest the pair. We will of course keep you informed about the outcome of the case, but you can rest assured that after this evening it will be perfectly safe for you to visit the groaning stone with young Gillespie without fearing anything as dramatic as a druidical curse."

We said our goodbyes and returned to the hotel. Later that evening, both Holmes and I made the journey back to London. Following his plan, Holmes made the necessary arrangements with Scotland Yard to seize the stolen chalk the following morning.

We were told later that the police arrested a Mr. Turnbull, who had arrived to collect the valuable consignment of chalk. He claimed to know nothing about the stone being stolen and was only too willing to confirm that Catchpole had been his supplier. Norfolk Constabulary later arrested Catchpole and Parsons who confessed to their crime when taken before the magistrates. They each received a prison sentence of two years for the theft of the chalk.

The case had not been one of our finest and the crime could hardly be described as serious, yet there was a certain pleasing conclusion to the affair. And for the recuperative effects of my short trip to Norfolk, I will always remember with some affection, *The Mystery of the Groaning Stone*.

6. The Unveiled Lodger

"You may be surprised to learn that we are about to be reacquainted with a former client, Watson! And one I did not expect to hear from again. You will no doubt recall the victim of the Abbas Parva tragedy in Berkshire?"

I stopped cleaning my old service revolver and placed it on the newspaper to my side. "Indeed, that would be the veiled lodger, Mrs. Eugenia Ronder."

"The very woman. She conspired with her lover, Leonardo the circus strongman, to kill her brute of a husband, and in the execution of their plan was savagely mauled by a North African lion."

I shivered at the recollection of her horribly disfigured features. "I take it that the letter you hold is from the lady herself? Is she still boarding in South Brixton?"

Holmes waved the letter above his head in a somewhat jubilant fashion. "The letter is from the former circus performer, but she has moved on from the humble abode of her landlady, Mrs. Merrilow. In fact, she has quite a story to tell. Remind me, when did we originally encounter poor Eugenia?"

"I believe it was towards the end of 1896."

"Then it is a good four years since she relayed her sorry tale. And I seem to remember that were it not for our intervention, she may very well have resorted to the poison bottle."

"Yes, and I'm glad to hear that she has survived to this point. At the time she looked to be ailing rapidly."

He took to his seat in front of the fire and relit the churchwarden which had been abandoned sometime earlier. "She has experienced something of a turnaround in her fortunes. Ordinarily I would provide you with a synopsis of what she has said, but I'm afraid that time will not allow for that. The letter indicates that she is to visit us at ten o'clock this morning, and the cab drawing up outside suggests she is extremely punctual!"

His supposition proved to be correct, for it was less than two minutes later that Mrs. Hudson gave a gentle knock on the study door and entered to announce the arrival of a "Mrs. Eugenia Cullen". I smiled momentarily, believing already that I understood the nature of her changed fortunes.

The woman who stood before us was tall, full-figured, and elegant. Beneath a stylish black overcoat, she was wearing a white puffed blouse, complete with lace collar and broad purple ribbon tie. Her matching velvet skirt was fluted towards the hem and on her head she wore a veiled hat trimmed with violets, feathers, and red lace ribbons. The thick purple veil covering her face was cut off close to her upper lip and she retained the perfectly shaped mouth and delicately rounded chin I had seen all those years before.

Holmes wasted no time in greeting our client and taking her coat, before inviting Mrs. Cullen to take a seat close to the fire. She seemed eager to talk, declining the offer of a tea and quickly removing her gloves, which she placed delicately on the arm of the chair before looking directly towards Holmes. I could scarcely believe that this was the same woman I had once seen sitting in a broken armchair in the shadowy corner of a threadbare room in South Brixton.

"Gentlemen, it is so good to see you both again. Mr. Holmes, you must have been a little taken aback to receive my letter – especially as my previous note to you contained but a short message and a bottle of Prussic acid!"

Holmes smiled uneasily. "We are pleased to have you with us, and I am delighted to hear that the world has been good to you since we last met. Your prompt arrival has prevented me from providing Dr. Watson with any details of your changed fortunes, so I wonder if you would be kind enough to explain to us all that has happened since those dark days in South Brixton?"

Our client displayed no reticence in responding to his request. "I am happy to do so. At the time I was awfully close to believing that my life had no meaning. My confession to you helped to change all of that. I determined that I would lay aside my misery and find a path to some sort of contentment. Little did I know just how quickly my prayers would be answered!

"Secreted away in Mrs. Merrilow's lodging room, I had the gift of time. So much so, that I began to read and write in order to fill every waking hour. I zealously consumed all manner of books, magazines, and periodicals. I took to writing short fictional stories about love, life, and the circus, and was successful in getting many of these published. And I looked for any opportunity to enrich my life within the confines of those four walls.

"One day I chanced upon a private advertisement in one of the broadsheets. It read simply: *'Widowed older gentleman who loves books, but has recently lost his sight, requires live-in lady reader who shares his passion for the written word.'* At first, I believed this to be a scandalous attempt to woe vulnerable women into promiscuity, but the more I pondered the announcement, the greater was my desire to find out whether it was in fact genuine.

"I replied to the advertisement and was delighted to receive an invitation to visit a Mr. Henry Cullen at an address in Arlington Street. The gentleman concerned was most charming and as part of my interview asked me to read aloud to him from a story of my choosing. I had with me one of my own published tales, the rendition of which brought poor Mr. Cullen to tears – moved, as he said he was, by the heartache of lost love and the pleasing nature of my voice. In short, I was offered, and took up, the position as advertised. A few days later, having given notice to a tearful Mrs. Merrilow, I found myself lodged within the townhouse occupying an airy upstairs bedroom with a splendid view of Green Park.

"Now, I would not wish you to think that there was anything improper about the arrangement I had agreed to. The spacious home already had a staff of four, comprised of a housekeeper, maidservant, scullery maid and gardener. Mr. Cullen's bedroom was on the ground floor. With his deteriorating eyesight, he had come to rely on them almost exclusively and rarely left the house or ventured upstairs. At that time, he was a little over sixty years-of-age, but youthful in his countenance and sprightly in his movements. He had worked previously as a literary agent and his extensive library of books - housed within an expansive study next to his bedroom - bore testimony to his lifelong love of literature. My role was straightforward. I would read to him between the hours of ten and eleven o'clock each morning, from two until four most afternoons, and conclude each evening with a narration for one hour prior to Mr. Cullen's bedtime at ten o'clock.

"My visual appearance mattered not to my employer. In fact, had it not been for the tittle tattle of the scullery maid, he may well have remained unaware that I had any form of facial disfigurement. I was received well enough by the other staff and was free to go about my business with a minimum of interference. When not reading to Mr. Cullen in the study, I spent all my free time in the upstairs room. On the rare occasions that I needed to leave the house, I would accompany Mr. Cullen into town in a hired carriage. This arrangement worked well, as we were able to provide a measure of support to each other.

"It does not take a great detective to work out what happened next. Such is the nature of the human condition. Spending many hours together and enjoying intimate moments through our shared love of romantic literature, Henry and I became inseparable. So much so, that one day he asked me to stop reading and made me a proposal of marriage. I did not take the offer lightly, nor did I attempt to take advantage of the situation. I explained that I would provide him with the details of my previous marriage and the death of my husband. In return, I asked only that he share with me what had happened to his wife.

"He agreed to the declaration of openness and we each told our stories. Mine, you know. In Henry's case, the tale was more traditional. He had married Henrietta at 31 years of age. She was ten years younger. For the first six or seven years they had been happy enough, although Henrietta desired to have children. And when she was at last blessed with the birth of a healthy baby boy, the poor woman had not the strength to go on and died that same evening. Henry was racked with grief and could not bring himself to look favourably upon the child. He made arrangements for the young Charles Cullen to be taken to an orphanage in Watford and provided a substantial endowment to enable him to be taken care of until he reached adulthood. Since that time, he has never seen his son.

"We agreed that our past lives did not alter our feelings for each other and set a date for the wedding. I have now been happily married to Henry for some three years."

Holmes and I expressed our congratulations. Once more, I asked Mrs. Cullen if she would like something by way of refreshment.

"Perhaps a small sherry?" was her reply.

I rose from my chair, only to hear our client reconsider her choice. "Actually, Dr. Watson, if it would not be too much trouble, I think I might prefer a *large* glass of sherry. You see I have not yet told you everything."

I acceded to her request and poured her a fair measure of Madeira. When she had taken a couple of sips of the fortified wine, she resumed her narrative.

"My husband has been the most supportive and devoted companion I could ever have wished for. So much so, that he soon became aware of how troubled I was about the injuries to my face. Our wedding had been a small, private affair, with only a handful of invited guests. I was able to wear a specially commissioned wedding veil to disguise my looks. Thereafter, Henry asked me if I would be interested in consulting a specialist surgeon to see what could be done to reconstruct my features. I had not previously considered that anything of this nature could be attempted, so readily agreed to the idea.

"Henry knew of a surgeon at Guy's Hospital who had successfully undertaken several operations to remove flaps of skin from one part of a patient's body in order to sew these over damaged tissue elsewhere. The hospital itself claimed to have completed the first of these *skin grafts* as far back as 1817."

I could attest to this and gently interposed: "That is correct, Mrs. Cullen. One of this country's finest surgeons, Sir Astley Paston Cooper, undertook that operation. And you may know that in the previous decade, other surgeons have pioneered different techniques for cosmetically reconstructing facial tissue - most notably, the Americans, John Roe and George Monks, and James Israel, a doctor from Germany."

"Indeed. I was told that while the surgery was still largely experimental – and not without risks – it offered some hope to patients with conditions like mine. On that basis, and with Henry's backing, I agreed to undergo several operations over a six-month period. And while the enhancements could never be described as picture-perfect, I have been delighted with the results."

With this, she began to lift the veil from her chin. I braced myself for whatever vision might appear, but soon found myself transfixed by the remodelled features within my gaze. Gone was the grisly ruin and horror of a missing face. Her pretty brown eyes were now framed within more familiar features. The detail was still crude and unnatural looking, but the improvement was overwhelming. Like Holmes, I was temporarily spellbound.

When I at last found the words to reply, I could only congratulate her. "That is remarkable! Truly remarkable!" This was more than a medical curiosity; for it was clear that it had restored Mrs. Cullen's confidence and something of her personality.

"Thank you. I now feel comfortable to carry out my duties within the home without wearing a veil and use one only to travel. The servants are used to my odd features, and do not confront me with that look of horror that I had become accustomed to whenever my face had been exposed previously. And it is a measure of my self-assurance that I now feel relaxed enough for the skin of my face to be touched by my dear husband."

It was a heartfelt disclosure which moved me greatly. Holmes, too, seemed somewhat emotive in his response, but business-like as ever. "As my colleague has articulated, this is an incredible transformation. And I can see that it has had the most profound effect on your disposition. But your letter hinted at a *darker matter* which has come to light recently?"

Mrs. Cullen let the veil fall across her face once more. "You are quite correct, Mr. Holmes. And it is really for that reason that I thought to consult you. The matter has nothing to do with my surgery and is more curious than alarming. Nevertheless, I believe that something is amiss and would welcome your enquiries into the matter."

"We would be pleased to assist you in any way that we can. But first you must furnish us with the pertinent facts."

Mrs. Cullen finished what remained of her sherry and then responded. "It was about a month or so ago that I had occasion to go into the potting shed which is inhabited most often by our young gardener, Eric Rayner. I was looking for a spare pot into which I hoped to transplant some of my favourite bulbs to protect them over the winter months. Eric keeps a supply of small containers on a workbench just inside the door. I picked up what I thought was a suitably sized pot, only to find a small, folded note within it. While I felt certain that the note contained some sort of message or direction, I could not discern what it meant."

Holmes was immediately inquisitive. "Was the note written in a different language or a hand you could not read?"

"No. It contained a series of numbers, separated occasionally by a space, but laid out as if to form some sequence or sentence. I considered that it might be a map direction or even a code to unlock a safety deposit box but could make nothing of it. In any case, I was not particularly concerned by the discovery, just a little curious."

"Did you keep the note or write down its contents?" I asked.

"No. Well, not on that occasion. But I will come onto that. Now, it was only a couple of days later that another odd thing occurred, this time within the house. I should explain that when we need to, my husband and I will venture into town, most typically on a Thursday. That particular day we had just returned in the carriage. Henry went into the study which adjoins our downstairs bedroom to put his chequebook in the bureau for safe keeping. While he stores no valuables there, it does contain all our legal papers. Having opened the bureau, he believed that someone had rifled through the documents - nothing was missing, but being fastidious in his administration now that he cannot see, knew from touch that things were not as he had left them."

"I am sure that is most telling," said Holmes. "Did either of you consult the staff about your suspicions?"

Mrs. Cullen frowned. "No. I would have done, but Henry was reluctant to make a fuss. He said that if it occurred again, he would have a word with our housekeeper, Mrs. Strickland."

"I see. And was there any reoccurrence?"

"Not that I know of. But then we come onto another matter which did make me wonder if some scheme was being plotted within the house. Last week we had once again ventured into town on the Thursday. The trip normally leaves both of us weary, so we had turned in early that night leaving Mrs. Strickland to oversee the arrangements for securing the house. Ordinarily she closes the curtains and extinguishes all the lamps, leaving Eric to bolt the doors.

"I awoke close to midnight with something of a dry throat and decided to get a glass of water from the kitchen. Stepping into my carpet slippers and wrapping my dressing gown around me, I lit a candle and made my way quietly through the house. When I entered the kitchen, I could feel quite a draught and was surprised to see that one of the hurricane lamps had been lit and the back door was ajar. While it was foolish of me to do so, I stepped outside the kitchen and looked around. I could see a light on in the potting shed and felt somewhat relieved, realising that it was probably Eric who was still up.

"In the still of the night, I thought I heard two voices, but as I moved closer to the shed could hear nothing further. By this time, I was halfway across the lawn, some fifteen feet from the shed. With the candle held out in front of me I saw Eric come out carrying a small lamp. He turned back to shut the door of the shed and then addressed me directly, asking if there was something wrong. I did not feel able to challenge him, and merely replied that I had been concerned to find the back door open. He apologised and explained that he had forgotten to put a new pair of shears back into the potting shed and was in the process of doing so before heading off to bed.

"Ordinarily I would have taken him at his word for he has always been a most reliable employee. But there was something in his voice which made me doubt him. Not wishing to alert him to this, I made my way back into the kitchen. But instead of going straight back to bed, stepped into the parlour and moved the curtains aside to get a good look at the front entrance. As I did so, I saw a tall figure in a white shirt and dark frockcoat climb over one of the iron gates in the drive and head off left down Arlington Street. It was the confirmation I needed that Eric had been lying."

Holmes looked at Mrs. Cullen most solemnly. "This sounds like a very grave business. Did anything else occur that night?"

"No. I climbed back into bed and slept fitfully until the early hours. The following morning, I quizzed Eric once again, giving him every opportunity to amend his account, but he maintained that he had been alone that night. I did not of course reveal that I had seen his compatriot leaving via the front gate. And the matter did not end there.

"A little later that morning I was busy sewing in the parlour and glanced from the window to see Lizzie, our scullery maid, heading down the gravel drive to the front gates. On the other side of the entrance was the same man I had seen only hours earlier. While my eyesight is not perfect, I was able to discern more of his features. He was close to six feet in height, with dark hair and a handsome face, and immaculately turned out. He was wearing a double-breasted jacket, waistcoat, trousers, and black tie, complete with hat and gloves. I guessed him to be an under-butler of some kind. I watched as he chatted briefly to Lizzie, before then handing her what looked like an envelope.

"When Lizzie came through the back door, I was waiting and said that I had seen the man at the entrance. She explained that he had rung the bell at the gate and when she had gone out to ask what he wanted, had been given a letter which was to be passed to Eric. I was curious to know whether she had seen him on any previous occasion. While she answered in the negative, she did confirm that Mrs.

Strickland had intercepted at least one letter some weeks earlier. Without wishing to appear overly dramatic, I asked Lizzie to pass me the envelope, saying that I would deal with the matter and requesting that she say nothing to Eric."

Holmes interjected. "Did you trust that she would adhere to your request?"

Mrs. Cullen had no qualms. "Lizzie is a straightforward, hardworking girl, whom I have grown very fond of. She does not always think before she speaks but is loyal and dependable. I have never doubted her integrity and know that she is highly regarded by Mrs. Strickland, who would also be quick to act if she felt Lizzie was not wholly trustworthy. Aside from that, it would be fair to say that there is no great affection between Lizzie and Eric. She is constantly scolding him for entering the house with muddy boots and creating extra work for her. The two have never been close."

"I see. And what of this envelope, did you attempt to open it?"

"Indeed, I did. The envelope was not sealed, so I opened it and removed the note. And when I had copied its contents, returned the note and placed the envelope to one side."

"Excellent!" exclaimed Holmes. "And did you ensure delivery of the note to Eric?"

Our guest chuckled. "Yes, he normally takes a break from his gardening duties at lunchtime. I found him in the potting shed eating a sandwich and explained that the letter had been hand delivered. He looked a little unsettled, but thanked me and took the envelope, without saying anything of the sender."

"Fascinating. Now, do you have the copy you made of the note?"

"Most certainly. In fact, I can do better than that, for I also have another of the cryptic notes which I found in the potting shed only two days ago. Eric had requested some time off to visit his mother in Tooting and I took the opportunity to search the shed in his absence. I found this new note screwed up in the bottom of a log basket. Fearing that there was indeed some nefarious scheme at hand, I took the precaution of writing to you and requesting this consultation."

She rose from her seat and walked across to the coat stand near the door. Retrieving both notes from an outside pocket of her overcoat, she passed the papers to Holmes who began to scrutinise them most intently. When he had done so, he passed one across to me, saying that it was the earlier of the two. In casting a glance over the missive, I could not see how he had managed to ascertain this but let the matter rest. In fact, I could not make anything of the note at all, which read: '12,15,15,11   6,15,18   23,9,12,12   20,15   19,5,5   23,8,15 9,14,8,5,18,9,20,19 – 3,3'.

"Pretty clear, eh Watson? This second note gives us some further indications of the plan in operation, but I will need to clarify a few facts before acting." He passed me the second note, which ran as follows: '12,5,1,22,5   2,1,3,11   4,15,15,18 15,16,5,14   20,8,21,18,19   5,22,5   -   3,3'. Once again, I had not the faintest idea what was being communicated but nodded sagely. Mrs. Cullen was clearly intrigued.

"Gentlemen, you have the better of me, for I could discern nothing from the numbers. What does it all mean?"

"You may rest assured that we will get to the bottom of this. I can tell you that there is no great mystery involved, but it is indeed fortunate that you have brought this to my attention at this time. This being a Wednesday, I will need the rest of today and possibly some time tomorrow morning to tie up a few loose ends. Watson and I will then make the trip across to Arlington Street tomorrow evening when I will explain all. I trust that you and your husband will be home from town by six o'clock?"

"Of course. I will make arrangements for you to dine with us at that time."

Rather unexpectedly, Holmes declined the offer. "Thank you, but it is essential that no one is informed of our planned arrival. In fact, I wonder if there is any way we could be ushered into the house without alerting the staff?"

Our guest was not in the least perturbed. "That is easily done. We have a side entrance to the property which leads into the study adjoining our bedroom. This is accessible through a locked gate which sits on the south side of the house. Only Henry and I ever use the entrance which is not visible from the servants' quarters. I will ensure that both the gate and the door are left unlocked shortly before six o'clock tomorrow."

"Thank you – that will assist us greatly in what could prove to be a lively evening." So saying, Holmes rose from his chair indicating that the consultation was over. Mrs. Cullen seemed content with what had been proposed and having thanked us for our time departed a few minutes later.

My head was full of questions about what Holmes had made of the letters and why he had planned such a clandestine visit to Arlington Street. I knew that his passing reference to the potential for a "lively evening" signalled that there was likely to be an element of danger. But in terms of further detail, I was to be disappointed, for with the departure of our client, Holmes had already donned his hat and coat and was making for the stairs.

****

It was not until lunchtime the following day that I finally caught up with my good friend. I had been busy attending to half a dozen house calls that morning and called in at Baker Street shortly before one o'clock. Mrs. Hudson was most accommodating in offering me a sandwich of thickly cut bread and cold sliced beef. As I entered the upstairs study, I noted that Holmes had already finished his luncheon and was sat before the fire drawing on his churchwarden.

"Ah, Watson! I see that you have finished work for the day and are already prepared for our planned visit to Arlington Street."

Knowing of Holmes's methods, I realised that the absence of my medical bag told him I had already stopped off at my home. And the bulge in the right-hand pocket of my overcoat provided him with confirmation that I had thought to bring with me the service revolver I had cleaned thoroughly the day before. As my hand momentarily brushed the flap of the pocket, I saw that he had followed my line of reasoning and was smiling broadly.

"I have made particularly good progress on the case - a simple affair, but a timely intervention. I doubt you will need your revolver, but it is as well to be prepared. The man we are dealing with is both clever and determined, and fully prepared to kill those who stand in his way."

I was surprised at the disclosure. "Then there is murder afoot?"

"I believe so. But we are two or three steps ahead of our would-be killer."

"So you know who he is?"

"Of course, as you would if you had deciphered the coded notes."

I felt a twinge of embarrassment as I admitted that the numbers had meant nothing to me, and I had been reluctant to say as much in front of our client.

Holmes grinned once again. "Well, you have plenty of time to make up for that this afternoon. The notes are still there on the table. I have one more pressing visit to attend to and will return by five o'clock. By then, I expect you to have cracked the code and be able to confirm what you believe to be the plot at hand!

He left me a few minutes later, saying he was to visit a property in Pimlico. I resigned myself to an afternoon of mental concentration, determined to show Holmes that I could make sense of it all. As it turned out, being left alone with only my own thoughts for company, I had it cracked within ten minutes and could but smirk at the simplicity of the case.

****

True to his word, Holmes returned to 221B a good hour before we needed to be at Arlington Street. It was mild outside, and we agreed to walk the mile and a half to the Cullen's townhouse. On the way I was able to explain what I had deciphered and what I believed to be the bare bones of the case. I was reassured to learn that Holmes concurred with every part of my synopsis.

"Splendid! I have but a few additional details to add based on what I have been able to find out since yesterday. I will share those with you when we explain everything to Mrs. Cullen."

It was a pleasant walk to our destination. We had some time to spare when we got to Arlington Street and spent a short while sat on a park bench beneath a gas lamp within

Green Park. At five minutes to six we approached the side entrance to the townhouse having entered through the small gate.

As we stepped into the study we were greeted immediately by our client. Mrs. Cullen wore no veil and seemed quite relaxed. She quickly introduced us to her husband, a tall, well-groomed gentleman with a pleasing countenance and upright stature. He welcomed us into his home and said that certain preparations had been made. Eric Rayner had been sent into town to purchase a new garden fork and was expected back around six-thirty. Lizzie the scullery maid had been similarly tasked to pick up a roll of dress fabric from a shop in Piccadilly. Elizabeth Cleary, the maidservant, was taking a half-day holiday to visit an aged aunt in Brighton, which left only Mrs. Strickland. She was busy preparing the Cullen's evening meal and was, in any case, the most trusted of their employees.

Holmes expressed his gratitude: "Thank you. All of that will assist us in our endeavours this evening, particularly the absence of your gardener. With that in mind, would it be possible for me to take a quick look within the potting shed before we outline the nature of this affair?"

"Most certainly, Mr. Holmes. Eugenia will be able to guide you there on a route which is not visible from the kitchen."

Our client responded accordingly and with a lamp taken from a table within the study led Holmes through a door and off into the house. In the time they were gone, Henry Cullen and I chatted amiably about art and literature and he confessed to being a great admirer of my narratives.

Holmes returned some ten minutes later. With the four of us seated around the fireplace, my colleague began to sketch out the facts as he had uncovered them.

"It is as well that you came to us yesterday, Mrs. Cullen, for I can confirm that your gardener is immersed in a plot to kill both you and your husband. My quick search of the potting shed revealed a sum of money hidden within a tool chest – no doubt some advance payment for young Eric's complicity in this affair. I also found a new cudgel placed conveniently on the workbench inside the door, which may have been purchased during Eric's recent trip to Tooting. I believe that to be the weapon which our assailant is planning to use tonight when he enters the house intent on assaulting you."

The Cullen's looked horrified at the revelation. It was Henry who spoke first. "Why would Eric want to kill us? If his intention is to steal from the house, he could easily have done that earlier today when we were in town."

"This is not a simple case of robbery, although it is most likely that the events planned for this evening are to be made to look like a straightforward case of burglary. And I should emphasise that Eric will not be the man wielding the cudgel. That role is to be undertaken by your own son, Charles Cullen..."

The shock of the pair was palpable. Henry Cullen was immediately tearful. His wife was breathing heavily and struggling to voice any sort of response. When at last she did speak, it was to Henry that she addressed her concern. "My love, it is not my place to judge you for the way you treated your son all those years ago, but I suppose it was inevitable that one day Charles might attempt to contact you. We could not have known that his intentions would be quite so iniquitous."

Her husband could only agree. "I fear that I have very nearly been the architect of my own demise. But how can you be so sure that Charles is the person behind all of this?"

"The evidence is set out on the two coded messages received by your gardener. Doctor Watson can explain what they spelt out."

I was a little surprised to be asked to elaborate, but relished the opportunity, retrieving the two notes from inside my jacket. "Your son used a simple letter to number cipher to communicate with the gardener, where the letter 'A' would be represented by the number '1', 'B' by the digit '2' and so on. Translated, the earlier of the two notes reads: 'Look for will to see who inherits' and is signed off with the initials, 'CC'. It helps to explain why the papers in your bureau were searched through a month or so ago."

Henry Cullen interjected. "Heaven's above! The will leaves all my possessions to Eugenia, but if anything should happen to her, the estate would pass to Charles as my only living relative. It was a change to the will which we discussed and agreed only six months ago. So, having learnt of the provisions in the will, you believe that Charles is prepared to kill us both in order to inherit?"

"Indeed. And the second note tells us when. Translated, it reads, 'Leave back door open Thurs Eve' and is again signed 'CC'. We believe that Charles is planning to visit the house tonight when everyone has gone to bed, including your gardener. The latter could then claim that he was tucked up in bed during the attack and not involved in the plot."

Mrs. Cullen asked: "How can you be sure? This all seems so far-fetched."

Holmes then explained. "The notes suggested that it was Charles who was behind all of the strange events of the past month. But I needed further proof. After you left Baker Street yesterday, I travelled to Watford. You had mentioned that the infant Charles had been placed in an orphanage there. The only institution of that nature in Watford is the London Orphan Asylum. Consulting their records, I was able to confirm that a 'Charles Cullen' had been a pupil and boarder there for some years. And having reached the age of 21 had left the asylum - the records showing that he entered domestic service working for a family at an address in Pimlico.

"I made my way there this morning and enquired after Charles. The butler explained that in his time working for the family the lad had proved to be industrious and quick to learn, eventually becoming an under-footman within the house. Some nine months ago, he secured a position as a footman elsewhere and handed in his notice, the butler being disappointed to lose him. He is now employed in a house only four doors away from here, further along Arlington Street."

"That would seem to confirm the matter," agreed Mrs. Cullen. "I suppose it was all part of his plan to get closer to his father."

"It would seem so. And I think we can easily surmise that he became acquainted with Eric Rayner to further pursue that objective. Having someone within the house meant that he did not have to risk exposure. And it's possible that he learned of the planned changes to the will from the gardener, who may have overheard your conversations."

"That is quite possible," agreed Mr. Cullen. "I have been a fool, Mr. Holmes, an absolute fool. Is it any wonder that the boy hates me so much?"

Holmes looked sympathetic. "I cannot answer that. But I can ensure that your son is prevented from committing the most heinous of crimes tonight. Watson and I will remain here in this study while you dine and play out the evening as you would ordinarily. You are to give the staff no hint that anything is afoot. And when everyone has retired to bed, we will be vigilant in waiting for your son to appear."

The couple seemed content with the plan. Mrs. Cullen then suggested that the door of the study be locked from the inside to prevent any of the staff from inadvertently discovering the two of us. We retained the key to enable us to make our way through the house later that night. She agreed to inform the housekeeper that the windows in the study had been secured and the curtains drawn.

Left alone, Holmes and I helped ourselves to some brandy and settled down for the evening, conversing in hushed tones. At ten o'clock we heard the Cullens retiring for the night in the room next door. Sometime later there was the sound of footsteps ascending the stairs which we guessed to be the female servants heading for bed. It was only much later, at around eleven-thirty, that we heard a final footfall – a signal that the gardener had turned in.

We allowed another fifteen minutes to elapse before quietly unlocking the study door and tip-toeing our way through to the kitchen. It was a clear moonlit night making it easy to see and having taken in the layout decided to position ourselves within the pantry to the left of the back door. Charles Cullen could not enter the house without passing within a couple of feet of the pantry door, which was open sufficiently to enable us to watch his movements. I already had my revolver to hand.

We had but a short time to wait for the young footman to arrive. There was the distinct sound of the doorknob being turned and the light tread of the intruder as he stepped into the kitchen and closed the door behind him. We watched as our quarry took three or four paces beyond the pantry. I could see that in his right hand he was carrying the cudgel.

Holmes decided to act immediately, opening the pantry door silently and stepping into the room behind Cullen. Quietly but clearly, he said: "Put the cudgel down, Mr. Cullen. There are two of us and my colleague is armed with a revolver."

Charles Cullen froze momentarily and then turned around slowly. His face betrayed a mixture of astonishment and anger. His eyes were fixed on Holmes who stood ahead of me. I raised the revolver and stepped forward. Realising that he could not take on both of us, Cullen let his arm fall and dropped the cudgel on the floor. "Who are you? You're not employed in this house."

"My name is Sherlock Holmes. I'm acting for your father and step-mother to stop you from committing murder."

Cullen snorted unexpectedly. "I can guess the rest. And I imagine this must be the renowned Dr. Watson? How bitterly ironic! My plotting was inspired by the tales of your adventures. It seems my literary heroes have sought to outfox me, probably with the help of that half-witted gardener."

There was no doubting that the tall, eloquent, and evidently well-read, young man stood before us was Henry Cullen's son. The angry expression had disappeared, replaced by a boyish smirk.

"Of course, you have rather placed the cart before the horse, Mr. Holmes. If you hope to have me arrested for attempted murder, I will of course deny that that was my intention. Having stopped me at this point, there is no evidence to prove that I had anything more than burglary in mind."

He was wholly unaware that someone else had entered the kitchen behind him. When Henry Cullen spoke, the young man was startled and turned quickly to face his father.

"You will not be arrested, Charles. Having seen to it that you were incarcerated for the first twenty-one years of your life, I am not prepared to see you languish in a prison cell for the remainder of your days. I blame myself for all that has happened and can understand why you feel such contempt for me."

It was a heartfelt admission which was met with a cold and vicious response. "Don't you dare patronise me! Not now, not ever. I would rather dance at the end of a hangman's noose than acknowledge your paternity. All I wanted was your money, which I understand you would rather leave to a scar-faced harridan..."

There was to be no rapprochement beyond this episode. While the young footman was to face no charges for his conduct that night, he returned to his place of employment vowing never to speak to his father again. Eric Rayner was dismissed the next day and warned about ever returning to Arlington Street. And while Mr. and Mrs. Cullen were grateful for what Holmes and I had done, they could not hide their deep distress at the events which had unfolded that night.

Mrs. Eugenia Cullen continued to send short notes and Christmas cards to 221B for some years after this. As a writer, her romantic stories had brought her some small fame, although she shunned public attention. With the passing of her husband in the spring of 1903, she once again became something of a recluse, refusing to leave the house and relying on the support of her loyal household staff. When she eventually died in June 1908, she ensured that all of them were well provided for. A small obituary in *The Times* marked her departure and described her broader legacy. The whole of her estate, then estimated to be worth around £350,000, was to be left to a charity which housed and cared for injured, sick, and aged circus animals.

About the Author

Mark Mower is a crime writer and historian whose passion for tales about Sherlock Holmes and Dr. Watson began at the age of twelve, when he watched an early black and white film featuring the unrivalled screen pairing of Basil Rathbone and Nigel Bruce. Hastily seeking out the original stories of Sir Arthur Conan Doyle, and continually searching for further film and television adaptations, his has been a lifelong obsession. Now a member of the Crime Writers' Association, the Sherlock Holmes Society of London, and the Solar Pons Society of London, he has written numerous crime books.

Mark has contributed to over 20 Holmes anthologies, including 13 parts of *The MX Book of New Sherlock Holmes Stories*, *The Book of Extraordinary New Sherlock Holmes Stories* (Conari Press) and *Sherlock Holmes – Before Baker Street* (Belanger Books). His own books include *A Farewell to Baker Street, Sherlock Holmes: The Baker Street Case-Files*, and *Sherlock Holmes: The Baker Street Legacy* (all with MX Publishing).

Mark's non-fiction titles include *Zeppelin Over Suffolk: The Final Raid of the L48* (Pen & Sword Books), *Bloody British History: Norwich* (The History Press) and *Foul Deeds and Suspicious Deaths in Suffolk* (Wharncliffe Books). His essays have appeared in over 30 publications, including *Mobile Holmes: Transportation in The Sherlockian Canon* (Baker Street Irregulars) and *Truly Criminal: A Crime Writers' Association Anthology of True Crime* (The History Press).

Copyright Information